A SLIGHTLY JONES MYSTERY

THE CASE of the HIDDEN CITY

JOAN LENNON

Catnip

CATNIP BOOKS
Published by Catnip Publishing Ltd
Quality Court, off Chancery Lane
London
WC2A 1HR

This edition first published 2013

1 3 5 7 9 10 8 6 4 2

Cover design by Mandy Norman
Cover illustration by Shane Clester

A CIP catalogue record for this book is available from the British Library.

ISBN 978-1-84647-1704

Printed in Poland

www.catnippublishing.co.uk

A SLIGHTLY JONES MYSTERY

THE CASE

of the

HIDDEN CITY

Everybody's heard of Florence Nightingale and David Livingstone. These books are dedicated to the nineteenth-century heroes and heroines who aren't so famous!

This one's for Gustave Eiffel, who built the Eiffel Tower, the inner skeleton of the Statue of Liberty, and more bridges, train stations, churches, gas works, theatres, fountains and viaducts – all over the world – than you could shake a stick at.

CONTENTS

✳

Chapter One:
What the Moon Saw

The moon was full, hanging gloriously in a clear sky. Two great cities sparkled in the night below. Cats prowled on the roofs of London and Paris, their eyes like tiny twin moons between their pricked-up ears.

In London, home of Slightly Jones, detective-in-training, there was no candle burning in her attic bedroom, no sign that she was eagerly reading the latest Sherlock Holmes story late into the night. Slightly Jones wasn't there.

In Paris, one ray of moonlight shone down, past all the attic bedrooms, down between the buildings to the streets where it found a metal grill in the ground, then down, further down, into the dark places under the ground ... A figure could be dimly seen, its face upturned, pale in the moonshine. For a moment, an eye gleamed. A hand lifted, as if to touch the light, and then the figure withdrew slowly back into the black, and it was as if it had never been.

Chapter Two:
Moans in the Steamer

At exactly the same moment, Slightly Jones burst into the cabin of the Dover to Calais steamer with her red hair flying and her eyes sparking with excitement.

'Granny, you *have* to come up on deck – it's amazing! The moon and the wind and the waves –'

'Slightly . . .'

'– and the boat's just *ploughing* through it and throwing up the water at the front –'

'SLIGHTLY . . .'

'– sploosh! Sploosh! And back and forth and up and down –'

'*SLIGHTLY!*'

It was at this point that Slightly realised Granny's face was a rather odd colour. A sort of greeny-grey. And she was lying down on her bunk, which wasn't like Granny at all.

'Oh, Granny. You should have eaten that ginger biscuit, like the captain said. He *said* it would help you not to get seasick.'

'Hate ginger,' muttered Granny. 'Hate boats.'

'Maybe if you came up on deck . . .'

'BE QUIET, SLIGHTLY!'

'I'll just sit down then, shall I? Until you're feeling better?'

If it had been anybody but Granny, Slightly would have sworn she *growled*. She decided that the smart thing was to do as she was told, so she curled up on her own bunk and started to read Sherlock Holmes' latest adventure. But then, after a little while, she stopped. And listened.

There it was again. A strange, muffled, moaning, wailing sort of sound. Like a ghost.

'*Oooooo . . .*'

'Granny? Is that you?' But Granny seemed to have dropped off to sleep.

Slightly looked under the bed. *This is ridiculous! Who ever heard of ghosts on a modern steamboat?*

'*OooooOOOO!*' It was getting worse.

She moved around the small room, listening hard ... *Is it coming from this side?* Closer, closer until she had her ear to the wall and ... *Yes, the moaning is louder here* ...

The knocking from the hall outside was so sudden it made Slightly bang her head on the gas fixture. Rubbing the sore spot, she scuttled over to open the door.

Mr Westerly stood in the doorway, stroking his moustache nervously. He was a big man and an accomplished artist, but at that moment he looked like a scolded schoolboy.

'Slightly, thank goodness! I don't know what to do ... The lady in the next cabin ... I'm afraid she is in need of assistance but when I tried to enter she – she threw her shoe at me!' He pointed at his forehead on which, indeed, a very small mark could just be seen. 'She insisted I send in her maid, but when I went to look for *her* I found she is ill with seasickness and I thought perhaps, if another female person – if Granny or you might ...'

'Slightly, go and see what you can do,' said Granny in a hoarse whisper. 'If I even try to stand up I cannot answer for the consequences ...'

Slightly slipped into the corridor.

'I'll wait out here,' whispered Mr Westerly, 'in case she gets violent again.'

Slightly nodded. She could easily imagine what this formidable lady would look like – very English, very proper, with an impressive whalebone corset under a bombazine dress and her hair all scraped back in an iron-grey bun. She took a deep breath, knocked on the door and opened it . . . to be met by a flood of French from an extremely pretty young woman draped gracefully across the bed, all silk and fluttery scarves and flowing flaxen hair.

Slightly stared. *SHE scared Mr Westerly?!*

The lady was still talking a mile a minute in French and it looked as if tears were not far behind.

'I'm sorry,' said Slightly. 'I don't speak French – could you tell me what's wrong in English?'

With barely a pause, the lady switched languages. 'Oh, yes, I can indeed speak to you in English and so I can thank you for your kindness in coming to me in my great sorrow. *What is wrong?* you ask and I can tell you in a word – Death! *That* is what is wrong! I am dying! There is no fairness in this – I am young, I am beautiful, I am *oooooooo* . . . !'

Ah-HA, thought Slightly. *My ghost.* 'I wonder if, just maybe, you might *not* be dying.'

'Of course I am dying – do you think I do

not know the cold hand of Death when I feel it?'
Nevertheless she looked at Slightly with a little hope.
'And if I am not dying, what is wrong with me?'

'Seasickness,' said Slightly firmly.

'What?! *Le mal de mer*? The sickness of the sea?'
She looked for a moment as if she were about to be
mightily offended – but then she stopped suddenly
and whispered. 'Is it possible? Might I live to see
another day? My beloved Paris? My equally beloved
husband?'

'Yes,' said Slightly. 'Here, nibble on this.' And she
handed the lady a ginger biscuit. The lady nibbled
obediently. 'Now, I'm going to take you up on deck
. . .'

But she was not so obedient about this.

'I couldn't possibly go out in public – look at the
state of my hair! It is in a mess!'

Slightly shrugged. 'My hair is always in a mess.
Here, shove this hat on and we'll pull the veil down
so nobody will know it's you.'

The lady giggled and suddenly didn't seem quite
so grown up any more. 'A disguise! You are so clever
. . . but I don't know your name. I am Madame
Araminta du Perche – but you must call me Madame
Mini because that is what my friends call me.'

'I'm Slightly Jones.'

'No. No, you are a heroine! An angel. You are Florence Nightingshade!'

'Er, Florence Nighting*ale*.'

'It is my English – you must forgive me!'

It was easy to do. Getting Madame Mini along the slanting corridors and safely up on deck with the way the ship was rolling *wasn't*, but Slightly managed and at last they were both giggling and clutching the railing.

Behind them, Dover's white cliffs had disappeared into the distance. Ahead, the lights of Calais were a sparkle on the horizon. The steam engine throbbed powerfully and the smoke from the funnel streamed away across the night sky. It was exhilarating.

'And now,' said Madame Mini, 'you must tell me *everything*!'

For one moment, Slightly hesitated. *I don't know this lady*, she thought. *She could be anything. She could be a thief or a con woman or a spy* . . .

Then Madame Mini looked at her and smiled her beautiful smile and said, 'I'm so glad I met you, Mademoiselle Slightly. To say the truth, I have been quite lonely of late.'

And Slightly's doubts dissolved. 'I wish you could meet my family. It's impossible to be lonely at Limpopo House!'

'Limpopo? That is a strange name for a house! Why is it called that?' Madame Mini asked, but Slightly couldn't tell her why.

'Nobody knows,' she said, 'except Granny. And she won't tell. It's a mystery.'

'I love mysteries!' said Madame Mini. 'And you and your Granny live alone in this house of mystery?'

'Not at all. And she's not really my Granny. She's my Great Aunt.' Slightly explained how Granny Tonic had taken her in as a baby when Slightly's parents died, but since everybody called her Granny, Slightly did too.

'Who is "everybody"?'

So Slightly told her about the Limpopo lodgers. 'Mr Gentler is a musician from Glasgow, and Miss Forth is a translator. She wears bloomers and rides a bicycle and she has a black cat called Cleopatra. And Mr Westerly is an artist. You've met him – remember? You threw a shoe at him. And of course, there's Mr Thurgood. He's a night watchman at the Natural History Museum and an amazing writer – it was through him that I got my first case.'

'Please explain to me what is "a case"?'

So Slightly told Madame Mini about her adventures as a detective-in-training: the intriguing case of the London Dragonfish – the surprising case of the Glasgow Ghoul – the terrifying case of the Cambridge Mummy. And Madame Mini seemed enthralled, her *mal de mer* completely forgotten. She asked a thousand questions, until the sun was coming up and the boat was about to enter the port of Calais.

As Slightly scurried off to find Granny and Mr Westerly, she found she couldn't stop grinning. She'd made a new friend, she'd crossed the Channel for the first time, it was her first visit to France and the beginning of a new case . . . (a sad and terrible case, of course, involving kidnapping – a very serious business.) But she couldn't help herself.

It was just so exciting!

Chapter Three:
Rumours and Whispers

When Madame Mini saw Slightly, Granny and Mr Westerly disembarking on to the pier at Calais, she gave a little shriek and rushed towards them, causing Mr Westerly to flinch in alarm. But it was not the beginning of another attack. Instead she was all apologies and charm, making much of the almost-invisible mark on his forehead.

'Oh, goodness me, I say,' said Mr Westerly, but Madame Mini had already moved on. 'And you must be the Granny who is not a Granny and who has been mother and father to my dear Mademoiselle

Florence Nightingown.'

Granny shook Madame Mini's hand and smiled wanly, swaying a little as if she were still at sea.

'I can see you have been suffering – ginger biscuits are the thing, I assure you. Come with me! We are in France now, and I will arrange everything.'

Granny made a weak attempt at protest, but Madame Mini would have none of it.

'You looked after me when I was at the door of death, and now it is only right that I should look after you.' And sooner than Slightly would have thought possible their luggage was taken up, they were whisked through the streets to the train station, installed in Madame Mini's first class carriage, and the train was heading off on its journey through the flat French countryside to Paris.

Madame Mini leaned back against the upholstery and heaved a great sigh. 'I think I shall never leave home again. I went to visit your London on a whim, well, my husband suggested it might amuse me, since he is always so busy – ' and Slightly noticed a sudden, sad look flit across her face, then it was gone, '– and it was delightful, of course. Charming! But I think I can safely say there is no place like Paris.'

'Have you lived in Paris always, Madame Mini?' asked Granny politely.

'Of course. And my husband also. Philippe's family has had the town house since the seventeenth century but I am doing my best to bring it up to date. And then of course there is the chateau in the countryside, just south of the city, and the hunting lodge, and a few others . . . it is a large work, getting them all refurbished in anything like a modern style.'

'You must be rich!' exclaimed Slightly, and then blushed as she realised how rude that sounded. But Madame Mini only shrugged.

'I imagine the city is much changed since I was there last,' said Granny, quickly changing the subject. 'It was a long time ago.'

'You have been to Paris before!' exclaimed Madame Mini. 'That is so delightful! And, yes, you will see many changes. That was the work of the always-so-busy Baron Haussmann. He spent many years knocking down the dirty old buildings and making new ones and new wide streets, most enthusiastically. And you are re-visiting Paris now because . . . ?'

Slightly opened her mouth.

'Slightly,' said Granny warningly. Slightly could tell she was sending the words *Think first!* at her as hard as she could.

'Slightly!' exclaimed Mr Westerly, waggling his

eyebrows. *Can we trust her? This shoe-throwing stranger?* Mr Westerly's eyebrows seem to ask.

Slightly waggled her own eyebrows as hard as she could. *Yes!* She looked beseechingly at Granny.

'Perhaps I will step out into the corridor to, ah, stretch my limbs . . .' murmured Madame Mini politely. No one noticed that, as she did so, she did not completely close the door.

'Slightly, is this wise?' said Granny softly.

'I think so, Granny. I think we could really do with some help. We've never had to investigate in a foreign country before, or solve a kidnapping, or battle a secret organisation like the Hidden City –'

She got no further. An agitated squeak came from the corridor and Madame Mini exploded back into the carriage, her eyes the size of soup plates.

'Did you say the *Hidden City*?!'

'SHH!' cried Slightly, and then more quietly, 'You know about it?'

'Yes. No. Just rumours. Whispers. My husband doesn't believe in bringing troubles home from work, but I know! I listen at doors and I hear things . . .'

'So it would appear,' said Granny.

Slightly didn't dare look at her. Granny had very definite views about eavesdropping and Slightly had got into trouble more times than she liked to remember for listening at doors and hearing things.

Madame Mini sank gracefully onto the upholstered seat. 'I can help you,' she said earnestly. 'Let me try.'

And, after a long pause, Granny gave a little nod.

'All right then . . . we're on a case,' said Slightly solemnly.

'I knew it!' cried Madame Mini. 'I have been so curious! What is it this time? Another priceless fossil? An ancient vase? A painting – or a statue?'

Slightly shook her head. 'No, it is much worse than that.' She lowered her voice. 'This time it is a person – a living, breathing person – who has been stolen.'

'Please, tell me everything. I will be still and attentive.' And Madame Mini put a dainty gloved hand firmly in front of her mouth to stop herself from interrupting.

'It began many, many years ago, when Mr Westerly was a student artist . . .'

'Steady on,' murmured Mr Westerly, but Slightly ignored him.

'. . . he was friends with another artist, a Mr Peter March, who went to live in France.'

'We lost touch, but I did hear he had been very successful – far more than I have.' Mr Westerly stroked his moustache as if to comfort it. 'Which isn't to say I'm not happy for him – he was always a fine fellow and an excellent painter and deserves every success that comes his way.'

'And then one day a mysterious telegram arrived at Limpopo House, addressed to Mr Westerly. It was from his old friend, asking for help. The telegram said this: *Maria kidnapped. Dare tell no one. Ransom demand signed Hidden City. Afraid.*'

'But who is Maria?' asked Madame Mini.

'We don't know.'

'Why does the artist dare tell no one?'

Slightly shook her head. 'We don't know that either.'

'And how big is the ransom?'

'Not a clue.'

'Wonderful!' cried Madame Mini. 'This is such an adventure – I will help! First thing tomorrow morning I will take you to my husband. He is a Trustee at the Louvre, like your Mr Gentler's brother in the Case of the Glasgow Gruel.'

'Ghoul,' whispered Slightly as Granny spoke.

'Slightly told you about that? I hope she hasn't been boasting.' And she gave Slightly a look.

'My Philippe will tell us everything there is to know about this evil organisation. You will see!'

An evil organisation and someone with local knowledge. This is perfect! thought Slightly. *Now I should get all of this down . . . a new page for a new case . . .*

She opened her notebook and prepared her propelling pencil and then spent a long time just staring at the page, her thoughts drifting about to the soothing sound of the train on the tracks. She yawned, completely forgetting to cover her mouth. She looked up, hoping Granny hadn't noticed.

Mr Westerly and Granny were fast asleep. Madame Mini smiled.

'Isn't it strange the way grown-ups do that the moment they get on a train?' Slightly managed to say, before she too dozed off . . .

. . . to wake with a start several hours later to Madame Mini's cry of, 'We are here!'

CHAPTER FOUR:
The Scene of the Crime

The Gare du Nord, Paris's 'Northern Station' was a chaos of steel and glass and steam. On every side, people were talking in French at the top of their lungs and flinging their hands about. Waves of noise seemed to hit Slightly like a hammer. All she could do was stand there feeling stupid, not understanding anything, until, suddenly, she realised she *was* understanding something.

Someone was calling to them – in English.

'Westerly! My dear chap – over here. Over HERE!'

It was Mr Peter March, come to meet them. As soon as he managed to push his way through the crowd, he and Mr Westerly shook hands enthusiastically and slapped each other on the back. He was introduced to Granny and Slightly.

Madame Mini, who had been passing out instructions to her maid and a small army of porters, gave a little shriek. 'Monsieur March? *Now* I recognise your name! I have heard of you. The Englishman who has made the most talked-about portraits of the finest ladies and gentlemen in Paris!'

Mr March bowed with a practised elegance and handed her his card, but Slightly noticed him cast an uncomfortable glance at Mr Westerly as he did so.

I wonder why? she thought. Then a large lady pushed past her, catapulting her into the path of a spindly gentleman who poked at her with his silver-capped cane. It was time to leave the Gare du Nord!

'I thought we might see if there are rooms at the Hotel Anglais,' said Granny. 'That is where I lodged when I was here last.'

Madame Mini went *pfff* with her lips. 'Oh, but you must not stay there! It is so stuffy – so English – and not in a good way. All tea and brown soup and let us pretend we have never left London! You must stay with me!'

But this was more than Granny felt they could accept. Fortunately, Mr March had a suggestion.

'I know a place you could stay. It is not fashionable, but it is respectable and clean. Unless –' And then he looked suddenly uncertain, '– unless you are perhaps a little superstitious, or nervous – some ladies are, I know, and I would not wish to upset you . . .'

'I can assure you, Mr March, neither I nor Slightly is in the least nervous *or* superstitious, and we *are* in need of a place to stay. So please make your suggestion.'

It was better than Slightly could have imagined. There was a set of furnished rooms to let in the very building from which Maria had been kidnapped! Apparently the landlady had been unable to keep her tenants since the incident.

The scene of the crime! thought Slightly excitedly. *We're going to be staying practically at the scene of the crime!*

'The landlady is expecting you. I told her you might be coming. I will give the cab driver the address, but then I must unfortunately leave you, to attend to clients at my studio for the rest of the day.'

'But . . . !' Slightly bit her tongue to stop saying, *But how can you go on working as if nothing has happened? Why aren't you out looking for Maria!?*

Mr March must have read her face because he leaned down and whispered to her, 'I need the money, you see, for Maria – I mean, Mademoiselle Leveret's ransom . . .'

Slightly was ashamed of herself.

'I can't say more here – it isn't safe. Who knows who might overhear? But if you would come to my studio tomorrow, when you are rested and settled?'

'We'll be there!' cried Slightly. 'Is six too early?'

'Yes,' said Granny firmly. 'If it would be convenient, we will call on you at ten. May I also have your card? Goodbye, Mr March, until then. Goodbye, and many thanks, Madame Mini. I hope we will meet again soon.'

'You may bank upon it, Mademoiselle Granny!' And waving Mr March's card at them, she glided gracefully through the crowds that parted as if by magic to let her pass.

Mr March hailed a cab for them and gave the driver the address.

'Till tomorrow!' he called after them, before being swallowed up by the bustle and rush.

Paris! thought Slightly. *I'm in Paris!*

Everywhere she looked there were wide, straight, modern streets and tall rows of buildings with pretty wrought-iron balconies. Omnibuses and carriages trundled busily up and down. Elegant ladies promenaded with ridiculous lapdogs tucked under one arm or tottering along beside them and occasionally disappearing from sight in the swish of their mistresses' skirts. The shops were full of hats and lace and gentlemen's waistcoats and boots and more fine frippery than Slightly had ever seen before.

'None of this was here before,' Granny kept saying, amazed. 'None of it!'

But then the cab turned into another part of the city.

'Ah,' said Granny. 'This I remember.'

It was a very different Paris. The shops here were small and dark and sold things like candles and cabbages. The people on the narrow pavements weren't sophisticated-looking, though some of them were certainly flamboyant. Slightly saw more than one person carrying an easel and bundles of canvases. She and Mr Westerly grinned excitedly at each other.

The carriage wound through the narrow streets that twisted and bent back on themselves, criss-crossing each other at odd angles, more like a maze than a city. By the time they arrived at their destination, Slightly was quite turned around.

It was a short, quiet street of tall houses and many doors, each with a different knocker.

'Number 4,' said Mr Westerly. 'Thank goodness the numbers are in English!' And he gave the knocker (shaped like a wolf's head) a vigorous rap.

The door was opened by a woman in a black dress. She was remarkably tall and thin with a remarkably long and thin nose. Slightly thought she looked as if she had wooden slats in her corset.

'Bonjour, Madame,' said Granny. 'Monsieur March sent us. We were sorry to hear you'd been having trouble getting tenants, but it is lucky for us!' She smiled pleasantly.

The landlady sniffed. She did not smile back.

'You are the English people. I am Madame Bec. I will show you your rooms. Two on the fourth floor with a sitting room. One on the fifth floor. You will have to climb stairs.'

'We are happy to climb stairs, Madame,' said Granny.

'And could we also see the scene of the cri – I mean, could you also show us Mademoiselle Leveret's room?' asked Slightly.

The landlady seemed to become, if that were possible, even stiffer. She sniffed again and looked down her nose at Slightly exactly as if he were an uninvited cockroach in a bowl of soup. But then something strange happened. Granny took Madame

Bec aside and spoke earnestly to her in such a low voice Slightly couldn't catch what she said.

Whatever it was, it had a surprising effect. Nothing could make Madame Bec actually unbend, but now there were suddenly two pink spots on her cheeks that hadn't been there before and she looked with a new respect and awe – at Mr Westerly.

'I am most happy to show you anything, Monsieur. Anything that might help Mademoiselle Leveret.' And she leaned forward in a wooden bow and led the way to the stairs. Then she added over her shoulder, 'I should have recognised at once, Monsieur – with such a magnificent moustache, what else could you be?'

'What's going on?' whispered Slightly and Mr Westerly at the same time, turning to Granny.

'I'm sorry, Slightly, but I told her Mr Westerly was a famous British detective – no, don't raise your voice – you could see she was not going to take to the idea of a girl detective, now couldn't you? And you wanted to get into Maria's room, didn't you?'

Mr Westerly stroked his moustache anxiously and looked at Slightly, who, after a struggle with her temper, managed to shrug and nod.

'This way, Monsieur,' called the landlady. 'Madame. Mademoiselle.'

She led them up a set of stairs with tiny landings, higher and higher until they arrived at the top of the building. Except for Madame Bec, they were all out of breath by then. The landlady showed no signs of exertion whatsoever.

She addressed herself entirely to Mr Westerly. Slightly tried not to mind.

'These are Mademoiselle Leveret's rooms,' said the landlady, reaching up to take a key from the top of the door frame and inserting it in the lock. 'I have touched nothing. No one has been in since the police finished tromping their great boots about the place. The mademoiselle has paid her rent up until the end of the month. I have never had any trouble with her. No rowdiness, no gentlemen visitors. No visitors at all, in fact. She was utterly respectable – the ideal tenant – and anything you can do, sir, to find her and bring her back safe, well, you should do it.' She sniffed, with emotion this time, nodded fiercely and stomped off down the stairs to prepare the other rooms.

'You first, Slightly,' said Mr Westerly, very quietly. It seemed right to be speaking in whispers.

Slightly stepped into the room. It was small and homey – all in one, a sitting room and kitchen, with a dressing table, a narrow bed covered with a warm rusty-red spread, and enthusiastically blooming red geraniums in the window, all tucked in under the slant of the roof.

It feels like my room at home, thought Slightly.

Maria's dressing table stood by the window. Next to a small lacquer tray for her hairpins, there was a circle of spilled face powder on the dark wood showing where her powder box had sat. The spill trailed to the edge of the table and onto the floor. It would appear that Maria was no more tidy than Slightly herself. It made Slightly like her, even though they'd never met.

She reached over idly, picked up the hairbrush, and stared. There was a hair caught in the bristles. Maria's hair. And it was red.

Undeniably, unequivocally, utterly red.

Slightly had an uncomfortable relationship with her own unruly red hair. Some people said that redheads had uncontrollable tempers, which Granny said was rubbish, but Slightly was always getting into trouble for losing hers. Other people said red hair was beautiful. Granny said it was what was inside somebody's head that mattered, but she spent time and effort brushing Slightly's curls until they shone. Slightly wanted more than anything in the world to be a detective – as great a detective as Mr Sherlock

Holmes – but she knew she didn't *look* like one. She knew what she *really* looked like was a ginger ferret. She wondered what Mademoiselle Leveret thought about *her* hair.

I'll never know if we don't find her!

'Slightly?' Granny called. 'Madame Bec wishes to show us our rooms now.'

'Coming,' murmured Slightly, but for a moment she didn't move. There was something. Something that made the detectiving hairs on the back of her neck stand up. Something someone had said didn't match up with something she'd seen. But she couldn't for the life of her think what it was . . .

'Slightly!'

Shaking her head, Slightly came out of Mademoiselle Leveret's room and watched as the landlady locked up and placed the key back on to the top of the door frame.

'I will put the young lady here,' she said, opening the door across the landing and showing them another little tucked-under-the-eaves room. 'Your room and the gentleman's are on the floor below, where there is also a sitting room,' Madame Bec was continuing when, out of the blue, Slightly felt her face crack into an enormous yawn. She was mortified. What kind of detective yawns just when the plot might be starting to thicken?

'I'm not tired,' she tried to say, but the words came out jumbled.

Granny gave her a look. 'I apologise for my great-niece's manners. The fatigues of travel . . .'

What followed after that passed in a blur. It would seem that Slightly's brain had a mind of its own, and that mind said, 'Enough!' She was dimly aware of eating some delicious bread, cheese and ham. She remembered protesting vaguely about drinking tea ('We're in France – we should be drinking coffee!') and then being bundled into the bed at the top of Madame Bec's tall house when the sun had barely set.

'I haven't been sent to bed this early since I was a baby!' she managed to protest, and then, in a room that seemed to be swaying a little as if she were still somehow on the sea, Slightly fell asleep.

CHAPTER FIVE:
Mr March's Secrets

The next morning Madame Bec brought them sweet rolls and coffee – proper French coffee – for breakfast. And then they were on their way to Mr March's studio in the fashionable district south of the River Seine.

He met them at the door as if he'd been watching out for their arrival. You didn't need to be a clever detective to see that he was terribly worried. Slightly could also tell by the smile wrinkles round his eyes – and his fancy waistcoat and the ample tummy it encased – that this was not his normal state of mind.

Mr March ushered them into an elegantly furnished waiting room and then stopped before a shut door, wringing his hands. It would appear it was not only the disappearance of Maria that was troubling him.

'Please try to not despise me . . . I knew when I telegraphed you that it would all come out. I can't keep my secret from you.'

'March! My dear fellow?' Mr Westerly was beginning to look really anxious too.

What on earth can it be, this awful secret? wondered Slightly. Suddenly she had a terrible thought: what if Mr March was a Bluebeard? She'd read about men like that in the Penny Dreadfuls. Bluebeard had lots of wives and killed them and hung them up in a closed room. What if Mr March had lots of women in the next room that he'd killed and then hung them up . . . what if that was what had happened to Maria? Slightly's mouth went dry.

The door was open now – they went through – and there *were* lots of women – and men too – hung up on the wall . . . but they weren't dead. They were photographs.

'There. Now you know. I am an artist no longer. I am a society photographer,' said Mr March. And he hung his head like a dog who's done something naughty.

But why? thought Slightly. *What's wrong with being a society photographer?*

'These are really beautiful, Mr March,' she said encouragingly. She wasn't just trying to polite – they really were. 'These are just like the ladies we saw on the boulevards – and those little dogs – they look exactly like the real thing!'

Mr March shuddered. 'Save me from those little dogs. Squirmy, yipping, nipping, ghastly BEASTS! Oh, how can one as young as you understand how it can happen, that for no good reason, we can fail to do things we swore we would? When Westerly and I were students together we had such ambitions – we were going to be pure artists, not in it for the money. Oh, my good friend, what must you think of me? How I have fallen, haven't I? But even an artist must live and I like to live and live well.' He slapped his ample middle and looked hugely sad. 'It all costs money. And these ladies have money – and they like me. They like that I let them dress up in exotic costumes. They like that I photograph them. Them and their teeny, tiny hounds from hell! And the men are just as bad, dressing up as Eastern potentates and swashbuckling brigands. And now I am more bound to them than ever, for I must, I must, raise the money for Maria's ransom.'

That's more like it, thought Slightly. 'Can you tell us about Maria, Mr March?'

'I will do better than tell you, my dear. I will *show* you.'

At this point, Slightly expected him to produce the ransom note, but instead he unlocked another door, hidden behind a drape.

'My secret studio!' he announced as they trooped in.

It was just like Mr Westerly's room at home. There was the right kind of light from the windows, several easels, the smell of paints and turpentine, and sketches, drawings and half-finished paintings everywhere. There was a difference though. Mr Westerly painted many different subjects – people and landscape and flowers and cats and pretty much anything. Mr March's pictures were all of *one* thing.

One woman.

'Mademoiselle Maria Leveret,' said Mr March, his voice choked with emotion. 'My muse.'

'What's a muse?' Slightly asked Mr Westerly quietly.

'A muse? It's someone who inspires you. Makes you want to paint, or sing, or write – whatever it is you do.'

Slightly looked at Mr March's muse. And looked again. Mr March was a skilful artist, of that there was no doubt, but ...

'She's not really very beautiful!' The words came out of their own accord. Granny gave her a fierce look, but Mr March did not seem offended. He tried to explain.

'Beauty – that's easy to come by. But a face like that – with such strength, such architecture – you only find a face like *that* once in a lifetime. Do you agree, Westerly?'

Mr Westerly nodded. 'Wonderful,' he murmured.

Slightly looked at the two men in amazement, but they were both tipping their heads to one side and gazing raptly. So she looked at the pictures again. She tipped *her* head on one side, in case that helped. She wasn't good at guessing the ages of grown-ups. A young woman, not a girl, and not old either. Mademoiselle Leveret had a strong jaw and cheekbones and her deep brown eyes seemed to be a bit too far apart and could even be said to bulge a little. And then there was her red hair.

Slightly didn't understand.

'She came to me as a photographic assistant,' Mr March was saying. 'I needed someone to help the ladies, especially those who wished to be photographed in costume. But the moment she walked through the door, I could feel the painter in me waking up again. It was as if my muse had appeared, not a mortal woman at all! I shook the dust off my easel, renewed my brushes, and, well, it is as you see.'

Mr Westerly put his hand on his friend's shoulder and said earnestly, 'You have lost nothing of your old skill.'

Mr March blushed just like a little boy. He looked so pleased and so sweet that Slightly very nearly gave him a hug, but still, she was confused. She'd thought it was all so simple. You were beautiful if you looked like the heroines in books – tall and slender, raven-haired and blue-eyed, or with silken hair the colour of wheat and skin that had never even heard of the word 'freckles'. Someone like Madame Mini. But now these artists, who were, after all, the experts, were saying that it wasn't that all. Bones – architecture – it was as if they were talking about a house, not a person!

Slightly gave it up. 'May we see the ransom note, Mr March?' She might not understand muses, but she knew what was what in detecting.

'Yes, of course. Here it is. Wait, though, I'll translate it. It says, *I have Maria. If you wish to ever see her again, do not come looking for her. Tell no one.'*

'*Tell no one,*' repeated Slightly. 'But you told *us.*'

'That was cunning, wasn't it? I couldn't go to the police or hire a French detective or involve any of my French friends, but what could be more innocent than a visit from my old friend Westerly here and his landlady and her great-niece from London? And what would be more natural than that these visitors would be going poking about the place, asking questions? Why, that's what visitors do! No one pays them any heed. Anyway, the last of the note says the amount of the ransom and that he'll let me know when and where he wants the money delivered. It was signed *La Cité Cachée.* The Hidden City.'

'And how much is asked for, Mr March?' asked Granny.

Mr March hung his head sadly. 'One hundred thousand francs,' he whispered.

'One hundred thousand francs!'

It was a huge amount of money.

'Do you *have* one hundred thousand francs, Mr March?' asked Slightly.

Mr March shook his head. He looked as if he were about to burst into tears.

'All I can do is try to raise the money and work every hour I can and gather together as much as I can and hope that the monster will come to some sort of terms.'

There was a knock on the door that made them all jump.

'No – it is too soon – I haven't nearly enough yet!' cried Mr March, clearly thinking it was the Hidden City come to demand their money.

'Calm yourself,' said Granny firmly. 'It is much more likely to be a client arriving early – or Madame Mini's curiosity bringing her to your door!'

She was right. There was a waft of perfume and Madame Mini sailed into the room wearing a very silly, very pretty hat.

'Have you spoken to your husband about the Hidden City, Madame Mini?' asked Slightly at once.

Madame Mini's face went sad. 'Alas, no. He came in too late and left too early – he is always very wrapped up in his work.'

Mr March stuttered. 'You . . . you . . . know about the Hidden City?'

Madame Mini put a gloved hand on his arm. 'Have no fear. I am Mademoiselle Slightly's associate. My husband will be too. This very moment, we will go to the Louvre and, how do you say, beard his den! Will you come?'

'No, I have clients coming. But please, dear lady,

my friends, you must be careful. If the Hidden City discovers I have spoken to *any* of you . . .' Mr March could only shake his head in worry.

'May I take this, Mr March?' Slightly held up a little sketch of Maria.

'Take it? What for?' Mr March seemed agitated by the thought.

'I'll bring it back! But it would be very helpful to me to know what Mademoiselle Leveret looked like . . .' He looked stricken and Slightly wanted to kick herself for being so tactless. '*Looks* like, I mean. What Mademoiselle Leveret *looks* like.'

Mr March nodded numbly.

We have to find her, she thought as they left Mr March's studios. *We just have to!*

CHAPTER SIX:
'The crack!
The crack!'

Madame Mini's pair of fine carriage horses drew them smoothly along the wide boulevards, but Slightly didn't notice. She was staring down at the little sketch of Mademoiselle Leveret as if it could tell her something, anything, that would give them a clue.

Then Madame Mini patted her knee and pointed. 'Look – *La Place de la Concorde* – the Place of Peace.'

They were crossing the river again and as the carriage swung round the great wide square, Slightly's eyes were drawn to the giant Egyptian obelisk that was its centrepiece. It made her think of Miss Gertrude Ponsonby and the Cambridge Mummy.

'I believe you have one like it in your London,' said Madame Mini. 'And there was a quite thrilling story of its journey to your shores, am I right?'

'Six men died,' replied Granny shortly. 'I don't think thrilling is the word.'

'Oh, dear, it is my English. You must forgive me!'

'Hmmmph,' said Granny, but Slightly could see she too found it very hard to be cross with Madame Mini.

But then Slightly forgot about ancient Egypt, ancient obelisks, ancient anything. Because, as the carriage turned she saw, there on the skyline, something utterly modern. Utterly amazing. The tallest structure in the world . . .

'The Eiffel Tower!'

'*La dame de fer* – the iron lady – she is impressive, isn't she? Though you can have no idea just how astonishing until you stand underneath and look up – or go to the top and look down!'

'Which we will certainly do,' said Granny before Slightly could explode with excitement.

'It's the tallest building in the world!' Slightly told Mr Westerly excitedly.

'Yes, I know,' said Mr Westerly.

'It's taller than the pyramids and it's made out of iron and it has two and half million rivets holding it together and there's this hydraulic engine that makes the lifts work and everything!'

Mr Westerly patted her arm. 'Yes,' he said with a smile. 'I know. I was the one who lent you the guidebook, remember?'

'*Arrête*! Stop the carriage!' As the coachman reined in the horses, Madame Mini turned to her guests. 'We will stretch our legs, will we? Through the Tuileries is the best approach to the Louvre and the garden is just coming into leaf. Spring is such a pretty season here!'

Obediently they all climbed out and began to walk. The Tuileries Garden was quite serious and formal. There was a wide, sandy way straight as a die down the centre, lined with tall chestnut trees with blotchy bark and the beginnings of green hairy pods in amongst the new leaves. There were fountains at intervals and statues Granny felt were not adequately dressed.

'It's Art!' said Mr Westerly.

'It's chilly,' said Granny firmly, and that was that.

Slightly saw more of Mr March's hated little dogs. They were staying close to their owners.

Too elegant to run about the place! Slightly was thinking, when something moved near her feet, making her jump back. A large, extremely healthy-looking, brown rat ran out in front of them, paused for a moment with one paw up, then scampered on. All the lap dogs studiously ignored it – sensibly, Slightly thought, as it was nearly as big as most of them. Still, she expected a bit of screaming from the ladies. It would seem, however, that not even the sight of a frisky rat could ruffle their impeccable style.

It mustn't be polite to notice rats in Paris, thought Slightly, so she did her best not to.

And then they came to the end of the garden and Madame Mini cried with a flourish, 'Welcome to the most important museum in the world!'

Granny won't like you boasting like that!

'Which part is the museum, Madame Mini?' Slightly asked as they walked under a great archway and on between two great wings of buildings.

'All of it, my dear. All of it.'

Slightly gulped. It was huge. It would take days to see everything in a such a place. Maybe, just maybe, Madame Mini hadn't been boasting at all.

'This way.' Madame Mini led them through a side door and along a high marble-floored hall full of milling tourists and on towards a grand staircase. Posed dramatically at the top of the stairs was a creamy white statue, all wings and flying draperies so realistic Slightly expected to feel the wind blow her own hair.

'The Winged Victory,' said Mr Westerly in an awed whisper, but Madame Mini barely spared it a glance. She swept along corridors bursting with wonders as if there were nothing out of the ordinary there at all. It was all they could do to keep up.

But it was not just guards and strolling viewers who filled the galleries. Everywhere she looked, Slightly saw easels set up and young gentlemen and ladies in smocks dabbing away. They were making copies of the masterpieces. At least, some of them were, most earnestly. The others seemed to Slightly to be more interested in whispering and flirting.

'Copying the works of the greatest painters is an excellent way for students to learn,' said Mr Westerly.

'Is he a student?' Slightly asked, pointing at an older gentleman who seemed to be making a lot more progress with his work than the others.

'No, he looks like a professional painter, doesn't he. He'll be making copies for rich people to buy. Someday, perhaps, photography will replace one painter painting the work of another, but so far, this is the best possible way to reproduce the glories of a masterpiece to hang in your own home.'

'Short of stealing it!' said Slightly with a laugh.

'And that would be impossible.' A new voice came so suddenly into her ear it made Slightly jump. But it was only one of the guards who must have overheard their conversation. He wore the official dark blue jacket and hat, and had the most enormous front teeth Slightly had ever seen in her life. *Part man, part rabbit*, she thought, and then blushed, glad that the guard couldn't read her thoughts. He gave her a grin that made his teeth look even bigger.

'Slightly, look at this,' said Granny, turning back to her with a pleased smile. 'I remember this painting well.'

The rabbit-toothed guard suddenly looked round and gawped at Granny for a moment before moving off to stop some tourists getting too close to the art.

Slightly sighed. Mr Westerly looked as if he'd died and gone to heaven and Granny was gazing about with a dreamy expression on her face, but Slightly was beginning to get a headache. So much – *too* much – to take in.

Focus, Slightly, she told herself. *Art later, Maria first.*

'Madame Mini? Your husband is here, right?'

'Of course! He is here. He is always here. This

morning he is showing Signor Vasarino, the famous Italian art expert, around the galleries. We will find him, yes, and then we will solve the case for you, Miss Detective Jones. My Philippe will know – he knows everything. There he is! Philippe! Philippe, my dear! I've something to tell you!'

An elegantly dressed gentleman detached himself from a group, which continued on into the next gallery, and hurried over to them. Slightly thought she'd never seen anyone quite so stuffy and starched in her whole life. He looked annoyed, and was saying what was obviously French for *Not now, dear!* when, suddenly, a terrible shriek echoed round the Louvre, bouncing off the marble floors and the vaulted ceilings . . .

'*The crack! The crack!*'

CHAPTER SEVEN:
Monsieur Du Perche's Doom

Slightly spun round wildly. Who had cried out? Then it came again, a dying wail,

'The *crack* . . .'

It had come from the next gallery. Slightly rushed forward, trying to see what was going on, but the room was packed and everyone was too tall. She used her elbows, the way London pickpocket urchin Matthew Bone had taught her, to weasel a way through the crowd. She practically fell into an unexpected empty space by the far wall, at the centre of which was a short, round, little man with carefully curled greying hair and an elaborate waistcoat. Nobody, it seemed, wanted to get too close to him. He was behaving in a most alarming fashion. His face had gone beetroot and he was pointing at a painting on the wall with a trembling hand. It was a famous painting that Mr Westerly had told her about, the picture of a lady called the Mona Lisa, but no one was paying it any attention at the moment. All the ladies and gentlemen were staring at the strange man.

'What is it, Monsieur?' Slightly asked. 'What is wrong?'

The small man spun round and grabbed her arm so hard it made her squeak.

'Oh Signorina,' he wailed. 'I come all this way to stand in the presence of the work of the master – and now – I am a famous art expert, Mademoiselle – I know everything there is to know about the Mona Lisa – I am Signor Vasarino – and now I am here and there! See! Oh I can't bear to look at it . . .'

'What are you talking about? What's wrong with it?'

The art expert was having trouble breathing. He swallowed hard and pointed at the picture again.

'The crack!' he whispered hoarsely.

Slightly looked. There was the famous lady with

her odd little smile and the strange blue landscape behind. 'But . . . I don't see any crack.'

'Exactly!' moaned Signor Vasarino, wringing his hands. 'Exactly.'

I think YOU'RE cracked, thought Slightly. The spectators looked equally bewildered, but that was probably because she and the Italian art expert had been speaking in English. She spotted Monsieur du Perche pushing his way through the gawkers, Madame Mini, Granny and Mr Westerly following right behind. Signor Vasarino saw him too. He let go of Slightly and grabbed Monsieur du Perche instead.

'Monsieur! Monsieur!' he bleated plaintively.

Monsieur du Perche wasted no time in bustling the agitated Italian off while passing reassuring comments to the crowd in French.

Monsieur du Perche wasted no time in bustling the agitated Italian off while passing reassuring comments to the crowd in French. Slightly, Madame Mini and Granny rushed after him through several more galleries and along a corridor. No one noticed that Mr Westerly lagged behind.

'My husband's office! Hurry!' It was clear that Madame Mini was not going to be left on the wrong side of *this* door. But when they arrived, the door was, in fact, still open, and Monsieur du Perche was standing outside, wringing his hands and looking distraught and helpless.

Slightly peeped past him and gasped. Monsieur du Perche's office was amazingly grand, full of ornate furnishings that looked as if they'd come from an exhibit themselves, and a marble fireplace, and a painted ceiling. Signor Vasarino was there, pacing up and down on a beautiful Persian carpet, muttering to himself in Italian and waving his hands about.

'What's he saying?' Slightly whispered to Madame Mini.

'I don't speak very good Italian, but I'm pretty sure he's saying the Mona Lisa is a fake!'

'*What*?!' exclaimed everyone except Monsieur du Perche, who said, '*Pas encore!*' and then clapped his hand over his mouth.

Just then Mr Westerly joined them, out of breath and shocked-looking. 'Oh, my goodness. Oh, my,' he was panting. 'I stayed behind to have a closer look – oh, I really don't know how to tell you this, but I think the gentleman was upset because the Mona Lisa on the wall through there isn't the Mona Lisa at all – it's a fake!'

He looked even more shocked when everyone turned on him and hissed, 'We *know*.'

'But how *do* we know? How does *he* know,' asked

Slightly, pointing at Vasarino. 'He was yelling about a crack and I said I didn't see a crack and he said "Exactly!" which makes no sense whatsoever!'

Mr Westerly leaned down and explained quietly in her ear, 'The Mona Lisa has a vertical crack from the top of the picture to the lady's forehead, where the poplar panel it's painted on warped. You have to look closely but it's there. Except it *isn't*!'

A crack that isn't there! thought Slightly. *Ah-ha!*

Madame Mini said, 'Is it the Hidden City who has done this?'

Even though she had spoken perfectly softly, her husband made a great shushing noise. He spoke in English. 'You - none of you - must say that name! How did you even *hear* of it?'

'Never mind how – do you think it's them?'

'Them . . . him . . . I have no doubts whatsoever. The blackmail notes have always forbidden us to speak of it, but now – now everything will come out and I will be ruined.'

'What blackmail notes?' asked Slightly.

Monsieur du Perche frowned down at her. 'And you are?'

'Never mind, Philippe,' interrupted Madame Mini. 'Tell *me* – what blackmail notes? Why did you say just now, "Not again!"? What *is* the Hidden City?'

'What? Or *who*? The Hidden City is secret and evil and huge like a giant web reaching *everywhere*, and behind it all, one man – the spider at the centre of all this corruption and dismay ... the one they call Monsieur X. Oh dear. Oh dear.'

Slightly felt a shiver down her back. *Monsieur X ...* she could see him in her mind ... cloaked, wearing a black hat ... his face only dimly visible in the shadows, but his eyes glittered and there was the suggestion of gleaming teeth and a sinister smile ...

But Monsieur du Perche was still whispering, still wringing his hands. Still acting afraid to go into his own office. 'Araminta, it's been *awful*. No one knows how it's done, but again and again, demands will appear on my desk, saying, "If you don't give me money, the world will know that such-and-such a painting is a forgery." And when we go to check, we find that it is true! Every time. Clever, amazingly exact, but undeniably *fakes*. So far, the demands have been surprisingly reasonable, so we have paid, and the paintings have always been returned. But now I fear we were only being softened up. This will be the biggest demand yet!'

Then they all heard Signor Vasarino's voice getting louder.

'What's he saying now, Araminta?'

Madame Mini frowned, concentrating. 'Now he's talking about going to the police – worse, he's talking about going to the newspapers! Philippe! Do something!' And she shoved him through the open door and into Vasarino's path. For a moment, the short man and the tall man just stood there staring at each other, but then the art expert poked an accusing finger at his host.

'The Mona Lisa is not genuine. It is a fake.'

Monsieur du Perche cleared his throat and after a number of attempts managed to say, 'Yes. Yes, it is. Well not exactly a fake – more a *copy*. That we know about. I mean, we know it's a copy. Of course we do, because the original is away being photographed and catalogued. I was about to mention this, but my wife called me away just at that moment. I am, er, desolated that you should have had such an unnecessary shock.'

Well! thought Slightly, her opinion of the stuffy Trustee rising. *That was quick thinking!* And Madame Mini immediately fluttered forward to back up the lie.

'Oh, Signor, I will never forgive myself. I am a foolish woman to have distracted my husband at such a moment but I was so *eager* to be introduced to the foremost art expert of Italy – dare I say it? – the foremost art expert *of the world*!'

I guess you do dare, thought Slightly as she saw the

little man nod in agreement. She and Granny and Mr Westerly sidled into the room uninvited.

'Of course we will have a viewing the moment the painting has been replaced –' said Monsieur du Perche.

'Monday,' said Signor Vasarino, drawing himself up to his full height, about the same as Slightly's.

'But . . . er . . . Monday is our cleaning day. The museum is always closed on Mondays –'

'Open it,' said Signor Vasarino.

'Of course, of course,' said Madame Mini. 'It shall be just as you wish. We will see to it. Philippe, send for a servant. Signor Vasarino needs a restorative and some pastries immediately. Who knows what terrible effect an experience like this may have on a sensitive soul such as yourself, Signor? But perhaps you might wish to spend some time recovering from this shock at our country house just outside Paris first? I think our new chef is really excellent, but I'd very much value your opinion on his work . . .'

She soothed and flattered and coaxed so skilfully that the art expert hadn't time to get a word in edgeways. A servant arrived with treats on a tray and Madame Mini settled Vasarino in a comfy chair and poked up the fire in the grand marble fireplace.

'If you will excuse me one small moment . . .' she said and darted over to the others.

Monsieur du Perche grabbed her arm. 'Araminta, do you think he believed us, about it being away being photographed?' Slightly thought he looked ten years older.

'He will believe us on Monday, when you have retrieved the original or found an even more convincing copy. Till then, what do you need me to do?'

'You must keep him from talking. If he does, even if the painting is restored, I will have to resign and the reputation of the museum will be tarnished forever. Oh this is a disaster! The Louvre is doomed. I am doomed!'

'Not if I can help it,' said Madame Mini, adjusting her hat. As she turned, she whispered three anguished words into Slightly's ear: 'Please help him!' And then she was cooing and fluttering Signor Vasarino out the door.

There was a moment of silence and then Monsieur du Perche seemed to suddenly become aware that he didn't actually know the people who were standing in his office staring at him.

'Don't worry, Monsieur,' said Slightly quickly. 'We are friends of Madame Mini, with some experience of detective work. You may count on our complete discretion and any help you might require we will gladly give. If I, I mean, we, could ask a few questions first?'

Monsieur du Perche dropped into the chair behind his huge antique desk and gave a helpless shrug.

'Excellent.' Slightly pulled out her notebook and readied her propelling pencil. 'First, are we *certain* that the Mona Lisa has been stolen? That it hasn't actually *been* sent to be photographed?'

'I would know.'

'All right, maybe somebody repaired it,' suggested Slightly but Monsieur du Perche shook his head abruptly.

'There's some bracing on the back to control the crack, to stop it getting any worse, but it's impossible that someone would do restoration work on the front without the Museum knowing about it. No, no, we cannot escape the truth. Someone has replaced the original with a very clever copy.'

'But that could be *anybody* – the place is full of people copying the pictures!'

Monsieur du Perche looked at her with an unnecessarily patronising expression. 'Don't be foolish. The masterpieces are called that for a reason, young lady. The amateur copyists learn, yes, a great deal, but they do not suddenly become great artists themselves. Any of us would have spotted a forgery by one of *them*.'

'And the professionals?'

'We have strict rules. They may make copies but they must be clearly larger or smaller than the original, so that it is immediately obvious they are not the real thing. Respectable people can make orders on the spot when they see the work in progress, or they can commission a copyist they like to reproduce a particular painting. It is a time-honoured and perfectly legitimate process and has been going on since we first allowed copy-artists in the Louvre which was, I believe, at least one hundred years ago.' All through this speech Slightly could see that Monsieur du Perche's stuffiness was returning with a vengeance. 'Excuse me,' he continued, 'but remind me just who you are, and what you are doing here?'

Slightly felt her own temper rise. 'We are here investigating a terrible crime perpetrated by this same Hidden City. Much more terrible than the mere copying of a painting. *We* are investigating the kidnapping of a *person*.'

'Who?' asked Monsieur du Perche.

'Mademoiselle Maria Leveret.'

'I don't know that name.'

Slightly drew Mr March's beautiful sketch out of her pocket. '*This* is Mademoiselle Leveret. The ransom Monsieur X is asking for her safe return is one hundred thousand francs.'

Monsieur du Perche glanced at the drawing and then put his hand over his eyes as if it were all just too, too much. 'Then that is it. I am ruined. The museum is ruined. If this devil is asking one hundred thousand francs for an artist's model, who knows what he will ask for the most famous painting in the world?'

Slightly was thoroughly disgusted, but then she remembered Madame Mini's whispered plea to her. 'Please help him!' *For your sake, then . . .*

'All right. We'll take the case!' she said grudgingly.

Monsieur du Perche looked up, utterly appalled. 'NO! Do nothing! Say nothing! I insist! No publicity – no publicity! You must give me your words.'

'But – ' began Slightly, but Granny intervened.

'It shall be just as you wish, Monsieur,' she said. It was only when they were back in the galleries that Slightly realised Granny had used Madame Mini's own words.

CHAPTER EIGHT:
The Watcher in the Street

High up, on Madame Bec's top floor, Slightly sat by the open window with her notebook in her lap and sighed. It had been a long, discouraging day, and now it was evening again. They had left Limpopo House on Thursday and it was only Saturday now, and yet it felt as if weeks had passed. There was only one day to retrieve the Mona Lisa before Signor Vasarino returned to the Louvre for his private viewing of a fake – a fake without a crack. No amount of flattery and fabrication was going to convince him this time.

He would go straight to the police, straight to the papers – he would tell *everyone* that the most famous painting in the Louvre was a forgery.

Not that it had anything to do with them. Monsieur du Perche had made *that* clear enough.

Too bad for him, thought Slightly. *But not nearly as bad as for poor Maria.*

It was one more day that they had not found her. One more day Mademoiselle Leveret remained the captive of the terrible Monsieur X. She didn't even know anyone was looking for her. How desolate she must feel.

This case – both these cases – were disasters. Slightly had felt so confident, so excited, that morning they'd sailed into Calais and now . . .

She turned the pages of her notebook, looking for inspiration, but all she saw were questions.

Why was Maria kidnapped?
Where is she now?
Is she all right?
Could there be some sort of connection between her and the stolen Mona Lisa?
What is the Hidden City?
How can you hide a city?

And there, on a page of its own, in big letters, the most puzzling question of all,

Who is Monsieur X??

Mr Sherlock Holmes had an arch enemy, a criminal mastermind, to contend with. Moriarty. And now she did too.

Slightly sighed again. Too many questions. And no answers.

It was getting late. Sounds drifted up to her as the sky grew paler – the sounds of families coming back to their evening meal, chatting and exclaiming and laughing at tales of their day. It made Slightly feel homesick. If she were back at Limpopo House right now they'd be doing just the same. Mr Westerly would be in the kitchen, talking about a tricky bit in his current painting. She could almost hear Mr Gentler's happy humming, and the sound of Miss Forth parking her bicycle in the back yard after delivering another fat bundle of translations to the post office. Mr Thurgood would be getting ready to go out to his work as a night watchman, full of ideas for the next chapter of his novel. And Cleopatra, Miss Forth's cat, would be wreathing around everybody's legs, meowling for tidbits from the cooking . . .

. . . And then, almost as if her thoughts had suddenly become real, or her ears had magically developed the power to hear right across the Channel, Slightly heard a cat calling *here*, too. Loud and insistent and eerily just like Cleopatra . . .

That's ridiculous. All cats sound the same, that's all. But nevertheless she leaned as far out of the dormer window as she could and craned her head back – the sound was from above, from the rooftops.

'Nwarrl! Nwarrl!'

Slightly twisted and peered and then she couldn't bear it any more and called out, 'Cleo? Cleopatra? Is it you?' thinking all the while, *I'm just being stupid – it couldn't possibly be her –*

And then she staggered back from the window with a shriek and an armful of black cat. Not Cleopatra. A young, strange, French cat.

'*Nwarrlll?*' said the cat.

Slightly stroked her fur delightedly. 'Nwarl? That sounds like Noir which is black in French, so maybe it's your name? Is that what you're telling me – your name?'

The cat rubbed her hard little head against Slightly's cheek and purred.

'I'll take that as a yes,' said Slightly. 'Noir. Pleased to meet you. I'm Slightly.'

Then multiple sharp claws dug into Slightly's skin. 'Oww!'

But it wasn't an attack. The cat was using Slightly to launch herself out of the window again.

'No – wait! Come back!'

But the cat paid no attention. She negotiated the lead slope of the roof as if it were a flat floor, heading for a window along the way. It was open just a sliver, but a sliver was all she needed and, with a flip of her black tail, she disappeared inside.

Slightly turned towards her bed, rubbing the pinpricks on her arms, and feeling lonelier than ever. And then she stopped and looked again. *Isn't that the window of Maria's room? But that window was shut, wasn't it?*

She frowned, trying hard to recall . . .

Granny stuck her head round the door. 'Bed time, Slightly!'

Oh well, thought Slightly. I must have remembered wrong. And she climbed wearily into bed.

⌒ ✳ ⌒

Something terrible was happening – if only she could get there in time to stop it – she ran as fast as she could, so that her lungs felt they going to burst and her heart was pounding louder than her shoes on the echo-y marble floors and still it wasn't fast enough. As she pushed open each grindingly heavy double door she found the room beyond already emptied and the doors at the far end just booming shut. Some awful force was sweeping through the building, taking everything and everyone with it, leaving only blank walls and sad whispers behind. She couldn't catch up — she couldn't stop trying — the place was endless, room after room after room and it was all her fault.

And then she realised the ceilings were getting lower and the walls were drawing closer, until she was no longer running through high galleries but passageways that grew lower and tighter with every step. No longer even a passageway, but a tunnel, shrinking around her, tighter and tighter, until she was barely able to force herself forward, barely able to draw breath . . .

And then she heard someone calling to her from up ahead, calling for help, and she knew without knowing how that it was Maria, Mademoiselle Leveret, who was begging her to find her . . .

The room felt stifling as Slightly woke out of the bad dream and the blankets were wrapped about her like a shroud. She untangled herself, staggered over to the window and flung it wide. She leaned out, taking deep breaths the way Granny had taught her.

In the nearby buildings, most of the windows she

could see were dark. From only a very few, slats of light escaped into the night from the rooms hidden behind the shutters. Slightly looked out over the rooftops, past the forest of chimneys – short stubby pottery ones, tall thin metal ones with little hats – to the sky beyond.

Where are you, Maria? she wondered again. Where in this huge city of so many souls was the one woman they needed to find? It seemed too big a task.

Slightly's eyes drifted down towards the street. It was late, and the clatter of feet on the pavements did not echo up to her. But the street was not empty. Leaning against a gas lamp was a man. As Slightly looked at him, he tilted his head. His face was hidden by the shadow thrown by his hat, but it seemed to her as if he were staring right at her. Watching her.

A cat yowled from the rooftops. Involuntarily, Slightly turned her head. When she looked back into the street, there was no one there.

CHAPTER NINE:
I Am Not Here

'Well? What have you found out?' Madame Bec asked Mr Westerly the next morning as she came to clear away their breakfast.

'Ah, well. Found out . . . Slightly, perhaps you could report . . . ?' Mr Westerly could paint anything you chose to put in front of him, but he was never very good at quick talking.

Slightly made a show of pulling out her notebook and consulting it, even though it contained nothing but questions.

'We – that is, Mr Westerly,' she began, 'thinks that Mademoiselle

Leveret's disappearance may be connected to some sort of secret organisation. There are rumours that this criminal circle is involved in widespread dishonest activities including art theft and forgery.'

Madame Bec made a tutting sound with her tongue and gathered up the coffee cups. 'I have heard these rumours, but nobody seems to know anything for certain. Nobody here has anything to steal, anyway. It'll be the rich people that you need to question.'

Then something surprising happened.

Just as the landlady reached the door, Granny called her back. 'I was wondering, Madame Bec, if you might know an artist by the name of Mr Charles Chant? I knew him many years ago and I wondered if we might go to him for information. He was a bit of a rogue, and if there are any shady dealings going on, he might very well be somewhere about the edges ...'

Slightly realised her mouth was hanging open and shut it quickly. Madame Bec was shaking her head.

'You haven't heard of him?' asked Granny.

'Monsieur Chant? Yes indeed. He was a naughty man, always in and out of trouble, but very easy to forgive. It's just that you'll get nothing out of him because he's dead. He's buried not too far from here.'

There was a moment of silence, then Granny said, very quietly, 'Can you tell me when this happened?'

'It was about the time the rumours of which we spoke were getting started. I heard he had got into debt.'

Slightly's head was humming with questions. Why had Granny never mentioned Charles Chant before? How had she met him? It was a long time ago – maybe they had been sweethearts? Maybe – and then Slightly had a horrible thought. *What if the Hidden City had approached this Charles Chant to do something illegal for them? Paint a forgery, maybe? What if he refused? WHAT IF THEY KILLED HIM?!*

'I would like to visit his grave,' Granny was saying. 'Put some flowers on it. It need not get in the way of the investigation – no one else need come.'

Slightly was torn. Madame Bec was the last person to see Mademoiselle Leveret before her disappearance and yet Slightly had had no chance to properly question her. Surely that was more important than visiting some old graveyard? *You can interview dead people till the cows came home but nobody ever solved a case that way. Not even Mr Sherlock Holmes.*

On the other hand, Slightly was very, very curious . . .

'I don't think we should let Granny go by herself,'

Mr Westerly whispered to her. 'It may not be a very safe neighbourhood – and besides, cemeteries can be sad places to be on your own.'

That settled it.

I can show people Mademoiselle Leveret's picture and ask them questions. Slightly had already found out how to say, 'Do you recognise this lady?' – it was '*Reconnaissez-vous cette dame?*' Of course, if the answer was more than *oui* or *non*, yes or no, she would probably not be able to understand it, but she'd decided to cross that bridge when she came to it.

Madame Bec pointed them in the direction of the cemetery and a tiny flower shop. They walked in silence for a few long moments as Slightly desperately tried to think of how to find out *everything* about Mr Charles Chant without seeming nosey, until –

'Well?' said Granny with a small smile. 'You'd better start asking some of those questions before your head bursts.'

Oh thank goodness! thought Slightly. 'How did you meet?'

'Do you remember the ladies and gentlemen we saw at the Louvre yesterday? The ones who were copying the paintings? It will be hard for you to imagine but once, many years ago, I was one of them.'

'Granny! I never knew you were an artist!' Slightly exclaimed.

'No, no, never that! But being able to draw, even badly, was one of the things expected of all young ladies. There were always mothers and aunties and chaperones in attendance of course, for fear that strange young gentlemen might speak to us. It didn't stop them, of course. There was a lot of flirting going on. It was fun – the whispering and the passed notes and the stolen glances . . . yes, well, it was a long time ago, as I said.' Granny had turned quite pink.

She's embarrassed! thought Slightly in amazement.

'He used to boast that one day *his* paintings would hang in the Louvre. And I believed him. He was so talented – he could paint in any style. He invited me to come to his studio, somewhere around here I believe, to see his other pictures too, the ones that he'd painted in his *own* style. But I never went. And –' here Granny hesitated, '– at this rate we're never going to get to the cemetery either.'

Slightly hadn't been paying attention to their route. The streets here wound in and out, curving round each other like eels in a basket, and she had now completely lost all sense of direction.

'Down this way, do you think?' suggested Mr Westerly.

Granny nodded. 'Yes, I'm sure you're right. Here we go – best foot forward now!'

They turned briskly into yet another narrow street. This was as far from the grand parts of Paris as it was possible to get. The houses were run-down and the smell of decay and destitution assaulted them from every side. Rickety children stopped grubbing in the gutters to watch them with sharp, hungry eyes. Greasy-haired women leaning in doorways and from upper storey windows cut their shrill conversations short to stare. Clearly, strangers were not welcome here.

What's the French for 'Excuse me, we're lost'? Slightly wondered.

But Granny wasn't giving up.

'*Où se trouve le cimetière?* Where is the cemetery?' she asked in her careful, quiet French. 'We are looking for the grave of Monsieur Chant the artist – perhaps you knew him?'

No one answered, and yet the atmosphere grew even more hostile. Slightly felt her stomach begin to knot up and stepped a little closer to Mr Westerly. And then –

'I will show you, Madame.'

A bent man with a stick and hair like an exploded hay bale had suddenly appeared at Granny's elbow.

'Oh – you speak English! How very kind . . .' Granny said.

The women went on staring, narrow-eyed, at them as their new guide hurpled off through the muck at a surprising speed. 'This way – this way! No distance!'

He was right. The gate to the cemetery was at the end of the next street. Slightly had been half-expecting something on a green hill like the Glasgow Necropolis, but there was no grass in this graveyard, only cobbles and tombs. It was below the level of the streets, built in the hollow of an old quarry. This time of the morning it was chilly and still in the shadows. Ravens cawed woefully and Slightly saw two cats curled tightly together in the doorway of a tall thin mausoleum. One suspicious eye opened from amidst the furry ball, keeping watch for danger. Still, there were trees, just coming out into their spring foliage. Women with their hair tied up in scarves were busy with little brooms and watering cans, tidying the dust off the family plots and sprucing up the pots of flowers just as they would their own doorsteps and window boxes.

'There,' said the straw-haired man, pointing.

It was clear that no one had been seeing to Monsieur Chant's small space. His grave was tucked in behind a row of grander tombs, quiet, unassuming, a little sad.

'*Je ne suis pas ici.*' Granny read the inscription. 'That means, *I am not here.*'

Mr Westerly explained, 'His spirit, it means, isn't here.'

Granny said nothing. She brushed away a few dead leaves and laid the flowers down.

Slightly felt it would be polite to move a little way away. She noticed that the hay-bale-haired man was still there, bent over his stick, watching. It suddenly occurred to her to show him Mr March's sketch of Maria.

'Excuse me, Monsieur, but do you happen to know this lady? Or have you maybe ever noticed her around?'

'Let me see . . .' He took the paper from her and made a noise of surprise. 'But this is good.' He peered closer. 'This is *very* good.'

'So you know her?'

'What? Oh, no. I just meant this is good work. Excellent work. It's . . . *inspired* . . .' He seemed reluctant to give it back to her, but Slightly went on holding out her hand until he'd passed the picture over.

'Slightly?' It was Mr Westerly. 'Granny's ready to go now.'

Slightly turned back, intending to thank their guide for his help, but he had already disappeared into the warren of gravestones. In spite of his bent back, he was quick on his feet!

They were quiet on their way home to Madame Bec's, each thinking their own thoughts. They turned into the street – and there was Mr March, fidgeting at the doorway and looking wildly about. The second he spotted them he rushed forward.

'They know!' he cried, his voice hoarse and horrified. 'He knows. I shall never see Maria again!'

Chapter Ten:
The Eiffel Tower

'Oh, how could I have been so stupid?' wailed Mr March as they bustled him inside and up the stairs to their sitting room. Slightly kept trying to interview him, but Granny insisted on making him some of the tea she'd brought from home first.

'Now, take a sip and tell us what has happened as calmly as you can,' said Granny.

'What does who know?' squeaked Slightly at the same moment, without sounding calm at all.

In answer, Mr March handed her a sheet of paper.

It was another message from the Hidden City, signed by 'Monsieur X'.

Your time is up. Put the ransom in an envelope and give it to the girl with the red hair. She will deliver it to me on the top of the Eiffel Tower, this evening, at sunset. She will come alone – or you will never see Maria again!

Mr March moaned. 'I was so sure they – he – wouldn't suspect. Stupid, *stupid.*' He banged his fist against his forehead, slopping the rest of his tea.

'Stop that at once,' said Granny firmly.

'The girl with the red hair!' cried Slightly. Excitement made her voice squeak. 'That's *me!*' She felt the hairs on the back of her neck prickle. 'He must have been watching us all along . . .'

Granny opened her mouth and Slightly knew exactly what she was going to say. She was going to say 'No. It's too dangerous'. And Slightly was going to miss out on the chance to meet this monstrous arch-criminal face-to-face, just because she was only a girl. Miss out on the kind of opportunity every detective dreamed about. *It's not fair. It's not FAIR!* Then Mr Westerly stepped in.

'I have a suggestion,' he said in a mild voice. 'I say

we do what the mysterious gentleman asks – almost. The Eiffel Tower is an *extremely* public place. I can't think that Monsieur X, even though he is a blaggard, will be considering any harm to "the girl with the red hair" there. It would simply be impractical. If he had suggested meeting her in a dark alley at midnight, then of course we would have nothing to do with it, but the Eiffel Tower? In spring? At sunset? There will be crowds of people there. I think with a little care – perhaps even a disguise or two? – we could mingle with the other visitors, keeping a close and careful watch on Slightly at all times, and Monsieur X would be none the wiser. We might even trail him afterwards, find where he's hidden Mademoiselle Leveret, set her free –' He paused for a moment and stroked his moustache. 'And if it's disguises we need, March here can certainly help. I imagine he has dozens at his photographic studio.'

Slightly turned eagerly to Granny. For a long moment she didn't say a word, just gazed intently into her tea cup as if she might read the future there. Slightly could feel the tension building up in her throat until, finally, Mr March spoke. Just one word.

'Please,' he said.

❧ ✳ ❧

As they stood beneath the mighty metal tower, Slightly shivered. Granny had insisted she wear her good coat and she was grateful for it now. It also covered her dress, which had acquired a rip in the sleeve somehow, making her even more aware of how well-dressed a crowd she was standing in.

The waiting was almost over. It had gone very still. The evening clouds hung, heavy and rounded, grey over the grey lead roofs of Paris and there was no wind to move the air. In the distance, thunder rumbled.

'Weather's coming,' murmured Granny.

An uncomfortable thought came into Slightly's mind.

'Mr Westerly,' she whispered nervously, 'aren't we going up a really tall metal tower? And if there's a thunderstorm, isn't that the sort of thing lightning is attracted to?'

'Well, yes, my dear, that's right, but I'm sure Mr Eiffel will have thought of that. They're bound to have put in lightning rods or something of that sort. I'm sure.'

I wish you SOUNDED sure, thought Slightly. But it wasn't really lightning strikes that had her stomach churning just then.

'Now remember,' said Granny, 'we'll be right

there. But you must try not to look for us.'

She couldn't see Granny's face under the heavy veil she'd pinned to her hat. That was her disguise. Mr Westerly and Mr March had ended up wearing slouch hats pulled well down to hide their identities. They had been keen to be much more exotic, but every time they'd come out of the studio dressing room kitted up as Oriental noblemen or Turkish pashas, Granny just shook her head and sent them back to change.

'We're trying to blend in, remember,' she said. The two artists nodded, but Slightly could tell they were disappointed.

'Be careful,' said Granny now, from under her veil. And then they were gone, up in the lift so that they could start mingling with the crowds at the top and becoming unnoticeable.

The next lift arrived, let out its passengers – and it was Slightly's turn. She handed her ticket to the attendant and moved forward into the heavy metal cage. As the great wheel groaned and turned, the lift began to crawl up inside the leg of the tower. Slightly looked across to the support opposite – the one with the staircase – and saw the not-so-finely dressed talking and laughing and puffing up all the hundreds of steps. The evening view from the Eiffel Tower was popular with families and courting couples, even on such a cloudy day as this. The ladies and gentlemen in the lift with her were more reserved, perhaps murmuring from time to time within their own party but otherwise studiously ignoring everyone else. Slightly wished she could be over with the happy noisy climbers, who wouldn't care about the rip in her sleeve, and had nothing more threatening on their minds than running out of breath.

For the twentieth time, she patted her coat pocket where Mr March's sketch had been joined by an envelope stuffed with francs, and reminded herself that she was a detective, on a case, alert and sharp-eyed and unafraid . . .

As the lift climbed, Slightly caught glimpses of the city, spread out like a sequinned skirt around her. *They must be lighting the gas lamps early*, she thought, *because it's so overcast.* Higher and higher it went until, with a judder and a clunk, the lift stopped and the attendant opened the door. They had arrived. Checking her pocket yet again, Slightly stepped out onto the platform in the sky.

It was crowded, as they had expected. Fashionable ladies and gentlemen strolled by, chatting casually in bored French or exclaiming in all the languages of the world at the wonder of the view. Over-excited children raced about, pursued by anxious parents. You really could see for miles, even in the poor light. Making her way to the railing, Slightly spotted the half-built Sacré Coeur, showing whitely on the hill above where Madame Bec's house was. And Notre-Dame cathedral. And the great green Camps de Mars and the Arc de Triomphe and the Place de la Concorde. The huge extent of Baron Haussmann's scheme of wide streets and fine buildings became clear to her. And through the midst of it, looking sullen and grey, the River Seine curved by.

Slightly wished she could just enjoy the view. She wished her breathing would slow down. Behind her, she could hear the clink of dishes and the chattering of happy diners in the restaurant, and part of her hoped that Monsieur X just wouldn't show up. *The cowardly part. You should be ashamed of yourself, Slightly Jones, you really should.* But scolding didn't stop her heart pounding uncomfortably hard in her chest.

Are Granny and the others here? Why can't I see them?

But of course the whole point was that she *wouldn't* see them. And neither would Monsieur X.

Don't look for them, she told herself. *Don't look for HIM, either.* She gripped the railing, stared blindly across Paris and waited.

Time passed slowly. It must be sunset by now,

but how could she tell? The sky was a strange, dark purple colour, like a bruise, and she couldn't remember which way was west. A sharp little wind sprang up that made her eyes water.

There! A jag of lightning ripped down the sky. Before Slightly could begin to count, thunder growled. The storm was very close. And suddenly there was lightning everywhere – painfully bright slashes right round the horizon and rolling thunder and a blast of cold air – Slightly blinked and shivered and, huddling her shoulders, shoved her hands into her coat pockets for warmth . . .

. . . and screamed.

Immediately Granny, Mr Westerly and Mr March were clustered around her.

'What is it? What's wrong? Are you hurt? What's happened?'

Slightly's appalled face was lit up by another flash of lightning and she cried out over the thunder – '*I've been robbed!*'

CHAPTER ELEVEN:

The Curious Incident of the Geraniums in the Night Time

'**H**ow? When?!'

'Just now. I was looking at the lightning and someone came and picked my pocket. It must have been him – Monsieur X! The money and the picture – oh, it's all my fault! Did you see him?'

But everyone had been watching the display in the sky. No one had been watching Slightly's pocket. Now they were no closer to identifying Monsieur X or finding Mademoiselle Leveret. And Mr March had no more money.

It was a discouraged band that bid each other good night. Slightly crawled wearily into bed. *What would Mr Sherlock Holmes do with this impenetrable case?* she wondered. Then she gave herself a shake. Well, he wouldn't give up, she knew that for certain. He would think. Hard. And then think some more. And he would notice *everything*. Not one, little, tiny detail that was out of the ordinary would be missed, and then he'd worry away at that detail until he'd built an entire solution on the basis of it.

Slightly blinked blearily at the candle on the wooden chair by her bed. *Don't need a candle to think,* she thought, snuffing it carefully and snuggling down under the blankets. Thinking. That was what she was going to do. She yawned widely. She was going to think until she fell asleep and go on thinking the minute she woke up. *The minute I wake up . . . the minute I . . . the minute . . .*

Several hours later, Slightly opened her eyes, sat up in bed and stuffed her fist in her mouth to keep from squeaking out loud.

The geraniums!

That was it – the one, little, tiny detail – the thing that had been tickling the back of her mind all this time!

'I have touched nothing,' Madame Bec had

said. 'No one has been in since the police finished tromping their great boots about the place.'

The room had been shut up. No one had been in. And yet the red geraniums by the window were flourishing and beautiful – not dead at all, even after all this time. How could that be if no one had been in to water them?

Shaking with excitement, Slightly threw on her clothes. She slipped out onto the tiny landing and reached up to feel along the top of the door frame. There! She drew down the key.

Slightly pushed open the door as carefully as she could. Its creaking seemed horribly loud in the still house. If Madame Bec heard breaking and entering sounds, Slightly would be in big trouble. She didn't know the French for, 'Don't be alarmed, Monsieur Police Office – I'm a detective.'

As she tiptoed into the room, the candle spluttered alarmingly. Slightly hurriedly closed the door, wincing at the sound, but the flame went on flickering and hot wax ran suddenly down onto her fingers, making her drop her candle with a tiny yelp. It hit the floor and went out. As she scrabbled about for it, she heard a strange, soft whoosh, like a sigh.

'What's that? Who's there?!' she whispered.

But when she'd found and relit the candle –

which burned quietly now – she could see that the room was empty. Slightly went over to the window. It was tight shut, even though she'd seen Noir the cat slip through it only the other evening. She pressed a finger into the soil at the base of the geraniums. It was damp, as if it had been watered only moments before.

Slightly felt a shiver go down her back.

Think it through, Slightly, she told herself firmly. *Think it through.*

Someone had been there and now they weren't, and Slightly had been down on all fours in front of the exit to the landing trying to find the candle, so no one could have gone past her or opened the only visible door. That much was certain. *And that can only mean that there must be another, INvisible one,* she thought. *A hidden door.*

Slightly raised the candle and stared at the wall in front of her. Then she stared at the floor. Then she stared at the wall again. It looked just like any other ordinary wall. It had cheap wooden panels and a thin skirting board.

She began to poke and prod along the edges of the panels. Nothing happened. She tried pushing both sides at once, in case there was some sort of double latch. She tried whistling and clapping her hands, in case there was a mechanism that responded to noise. She was sure she'd read about something like that.

Still nothing.

There's a door here — I know it! But where's the latch? Where IS it? Slightly's temper snapped and she kicked the skirting board and turned to go.

That was when she heard the sighing *swish* of the panel in the wall sliding sideways.

She turned back and there it was. A door. It opened into a narrow, shadowy landing. And, leading downwards, stairs . . .

Slightly hesitated only for a split second. She pulled her notebook out of her pocket and shoved it into the gap, in case the door slid shut and she couldn't find the handle on this side. Then, shielding the candle flame with her hand, she began her descent. The clatter of her footsteps echoed hollowly until they died away.

Then, in the hidden landing at the top of the stairs, something happened that Slightly had not anticipated.

A figure stepped out of the shadows. He was muffled in a black cloak, wearing a black slouch hat . . . His face was only dimly visible, but his eyes glittered and there was the suggestion of gleaming teeth and a sinister smile.

He walked over to the hidden door to Maria's room and calmly removed Slightly's notebook. The panel closed with a sigh. It was as if it had never been opened at all.

Then he followed Slightly down.

⁂

The stairs coiled tightly, each wedge-shaped step barely deep enough for her feet. The candle cast strange distorted shadows, confusing rather than revealing anything. She clung to the wall and tried not to think about how far she would fall and how much damage she would do to herself if she slipped.

Without consciously deciding to do so, she found herself counting – one, two, three . . . twenty-five, twenty-six . . . fifty-eight, fifty-nine . . . one hundred, one hundred and one . . . The air grew colder and damper. She knew she must be under the ground by now, going deeper and deeper with every step. Two hundred and ten, two hundred and eleven . . .

And then, so suddenly her knees buckled and she almost fell, she was at the bottom. Two hundred and twenty-seven steps down. Slightly lifted her candle and stared. She was in a low-roofed gallery cut out of the stone. She could see the marks of chisels on the rough walls. Five tunnels gaped like black mouths and she was staring from one to the next, unable to guess which one she should go down, when suddenly she was grabbed from behind and a swathe of rough cloth was flung over her head, entangling her in its folds.

'That's far enough, young mademoiselle,' said a man's voice, and before she could react her hands were tied behind her back and she was being twirled, round and round until she was dizzy. Strong hands kept her upright.

'That should do it. You'd need to be some kind of circus act to know which way is which now. You aren't some kind of circus act, are you?'

'Let go of me!' shouted Slightly but when the hands did just that, she staggered and almost fell until they caught hold of her again.

'Careful what you wish for,' said the man. 'Come on. Let's be on our way before anyone else uninvited decides to drop in.' He shoved her forward, keeping a hand on her shoulder.

'Where are you taking me? Who are you?' Slightly's voice quavered. She couldn't help it.

'Where am I taking you? You'll find out soon enough. And who am I? You can call me Monsieur X.'

Chapter Twelve:
Monsieur X

Slightly's heart lurched. This was the sinister, enigmatic man who had kidnapped Mademoiselle Leveret and stolen the Mona Lisa; who made grown men like Monsieur du Perche look over their shoulders in fear; the key to the case – the man she'd been trying to find. Except she hadn't found him. *He'd* found *her*.

'You won't get away with this! My friends know where I am. They'll be looking for me. You've bitten off more than you can chew this time, Monsieur X.'

'Do you think so?'The man's voice sounded more amused than afraid. 'I think you overestimate your friends. Oh, by the way, I closed the hidden door. Tidier that way. I'll just pop your notebook back in your pocket, shall I? Off we go!'

She had no idea which tunnel they entered or what direction they were heading in. She could not have been more lost if she'd been stranded on the dark side of the moon. *Sherlock Holmes would know,* she told herself. *He wouldn't need to be able to see – he would be able to tell where he was just by the smell of the air or the slipperiness of the stone underfoot.* But all Slightly knew was that the stones *were* slippery – scarily so – and all she could smell was a musty mouldiness from the cloak over her head that was making her feel sick. She stumbled on and tried not to cry, especially when she suddenly thought where they might be going.

'Are – are you taking me into the Catacombs?' She'd read in Mr Westerly's guidebook about the tunnels under Paris that were filled floor to ceiling with human bones. It had given her a delightful shivery feeling then. It wasn't delightful now.

'Scared of dead people, are you?'

Slightly swallowed hard. 'Of course not. Dead people can't hurt you.' She was sure she didn't quaver when she said this, but for some reason her captor seemed to find her words entertaining.

What if he's crazy? she thought, and blinked back sudden tears.

She stumbled on for what seemed like hours until, abruptly, he told her to stop.

'Wait there.'

Where was she? What was around her? Grinning skulls? Heaps of leg bones and arm bones and clutching finger bones? *Don't scream*, she told herself. *Just don't scream.* And then –

And then, Slightly heard the incongruous creak of a door opening and light shone through the weave of the cloth over her face.

'Uncle! Where have you been?' It was a woman's voice, speaking in perfect English.

'Covering your tracks, my girl.'

'What do you mean?' the woman said. 'No one saw me – and besides, the door is too well hidden. No one could find it.'

'Really? Then I wonder who that is out in the tunnel?'

'What? Uncle, what have you done?'

'She followed you down the stairs and *I* followed *her* and then I brought her here. What else could I do? Would you prefer she wandered about until she died? You who have caused this dilemma because you couldn't even bear to let your foolish geraniums perish?'

'But that's practically kidnapping!'

'And it's not the first time, either!' yelled Slightly as loudly as her dry throat would allow. 'He already kidnapped a lady called Maria Leveret – did he tell you about *that*?'

There was a sudden silence. Then the sound of a chair being knocked over as someone came rushing out, someone who exclaimed in horror and began untying Slightly's hands and releasing her from the musty folds of the cloak. The light from the doorway was painfully bright after being muffled up like that. Slightly squinted. There was a young woman with big brown eyes and red hair, looking at her with concern.

'But you're only a child!' the woman said, leading Slightly forward into an astonishing room. It was cut out of the rock, had a hearth with a fire glowing in it, a black cat asleep on a rug – *but that's Noir!* her brain exclaimed – a basket of knitting and tables and easels and the unmistakable smell of paint. All this Slightly barely noticed, for she was seeing something else that was even *more* amazing.

'You're Maria!' croaked Slightly, clutching the

lady's arm. 'Mademoiselle Leveret! It's you! I've found you!'

The young woman frowned, confused. 'I'm Maria Leveret, yes, but I haven't been lost. Or kidnapped.'

'Yes, you have – by him! By the evil arch-criminal master-villain, Monsieur X.' Slightly pointed at Monsieur X, standing in the doorway, but her finger wavered a little. Now that she could get a good look at him, he was a lot older than she'd expected and a lot more . . . *ordinary*.

Mademoiselle Leveret took Slightly's cold hands between her two warm ones and began rubbing them. She looked over at Monsieur X.

'What have you been telling her? Don't worry, my dear, he's not a master-villain. He's my uncle. My mother's brother. We moved to England, but when she heard he wasn't well, she sent me to see if I could help.'

'Of *course* he's a master-villain,' cried Slightly. 'He can be evil even if he *is* your uncle.'

But Maria shook her head. 'Naughty, perhaps, but not actually evil. He's an artist. He's Charles Chant.'

'Charles Xavier Chant – that's where I got the X from,' added Monsieur X.

Slightly felt as if her head were spinning round on her shoulders and sat down suddenly. 'But you can't be Charles Chant. He's dead! Charles Chant was a friend of my Granny and I think he was most likely killed by the Hidden City because he wouldn't co-operate with their evil schemes.'

'What is she talking about, Uncle?' asked Mademoiselle Leveret.

'We saw his grave!' Slightly insisted. 'Granny put flowers on it. She was *sad*! There was a tombstone and an inscription and everything . . .' A thought was dawning in Slightly's mind but it was unbelievable.

'Do you remember what the inscription said?' asked Monsieur X.

'It said, *I Am Not Here* . . .' said Slightly. 'OH!' She shook an outraged finger at him. 'You lied. On a *tombstone*!' That made it even worse.

'Well, no. Not a lie. I really wasn't there.'

'Uncle.' Mademoiselle Leveret's voice had steel in it now. '*What have you done?*'

Monsieur X hung his head. 'I had a lot of debts.'

'Then who is the real Monsieur X?' demanded Slightly. 'The one who's been terrorizing Paris with blackmail and ransom demands. The real head of the Hidden City?'

'Ah,' said Monsieur X. 'I used my real name for that one too. My initials – CC – for la Cité Cachée, which is the Hidden City in French. It doesn't exist

- well, of course, we're in the Hidden City right now. The underground part of Paris is called the Hidden City. But a secret criminal organisation? I just made that up.'

Slightly stared at him. 'But *why*?'

'When I was young – many years ago, when I knew your Granny – I used to boast that one day my paintings would hang in the Louvre, but of course that never happened. The Trustees are snobs. To them, the only good painter is a dead painter.'

'So . . . you pretended to be dead to get them to like your pictures?'

'No, I pretended to be dead to escape paying my debts.'

Slightly thought of the almost perfect copy of the Mona Lisa. 'But you decided to hang your paintings in the Louvre anyway . . .'

Monsieur X's grin was shameless. 'Yes. And then I charged them for it!'

'You *blackmailed* them!'

He shrugged. 'I never asked for much and they could afford it. And all the while, no one could pin anything on me. Who would suspect a dead man? It was brilliant – the perfect alibi!'

Maria was shaking her head. 'That money – you said it was from selling your copies of the masters.'

'Renting them, really,' murmured Monsieur X.

'You said you were selling all of them to get out of debt, except for . . .' And she walked over to one of the easels and drew away the cloth.

It was a picture Slightly had seen before – or, at any rate, a very good copy of it. The Mona Lisa. And there was the crack. 'There's no crack in the copy,' she couldn't help saying.

'Yes, it was unprofessional, I know, to leave it out,' replied Monsieur X, 'but I've never liked that crack. It was not part of the master's vision – I think he would have been appalled! Most people just don't see it, but Vasarino, well, of course *he* would notice.'

Then Maria, without a word, unveiled the next easel, and Slightly forgot all about cracks.

This painting was . . . breath-taking. Astonishing. It was Maria, sitting in the same pose as the Mona Lisa, but looking utterly different. Utterly herself. Even unfinished, Slightly knew it was a masterpiece.

'Uncle, look at me.' Monsieur X turned reluctantly towards his niece. 'You told me you needed your copy of the Mona Lisa to make sure I was in the right position. But this isn't a copy, is it, Uncle? You stole the real Mona Lisa.'

He shrugged. 'Charles Chant the artist painted

the copy and Monsieur X the master criminal lifted the original.'

Mademoiselle Leveret turned to Slightly as if she couldn't bear to look at him another moment. 'Miss Jones, you must be wondering how I can have been so stupid. I was sorry for him. And I promised my mother I would try to help. He *said* he had a bad heart.'

'But, Maria, it's true,' bleated Monsieur X. 'The doctors said so –'

She continued as if he hadn't spoken. 'And now, I find out that there has been nothing but lies.'

'It was just a game,' he muttered sulkily. 'It's not as if they didn't have lots of money to spare. Nobody got hurt.'

'It wasn't a game. It was blackmail.' She folded her knitting and began putting it into its bag. 'It was dirty. If I'd known about it in the first place, then I wouldn't have had anything to do with you. No matter what I promised my mother.'

'Maria!' Monsieur X looked genuinely shocked. 'You don't mean it!'

'Even if Mr March doesn't want me back, I will return to the surface and find another position.'

'What?' interrupted Slightly. 'But Mr March is *desperate* to have you back! He's been going crazy with worry and he's doing everything he can to raise the ransom money but a hundred thousands francs is a lot of money and . . .' She saw the look on Maria's face. *Oh dear.*

Mademoiselle Leveret's voice was dangerously quiet. 'Uncle. You told me you delivered my note to Monsieur March, telling him I would be away for a little while. You didn't, did you? Instead, you tried to buy me.'

'For a hundred thousand francs, Maria!' squeaked Monsieur X. 'And you're worth far more than that – to me you are priceless . . .'

'You must have known he didn't have that kind of money.'

'You're right – there wasn't nearly that in the envelope I pinched from Miss Jones. But that's not the point. I wanted you to think he didn't care. So you'd stay with *me.*'

Mademoiselle Leveret stood up and then, just for a moment, Slightly saw what the artists saw – the way the firelight illuminated the shape of her head, the strong curve of her cheek and brow, catching the deep auburn colours in her hair, the shadow in the hollow of her throat. She was furious and majestic and beautiful in a way that had nothing to do with being pretty.

'Give me the envelope, Uncle,' she said. 'I'm leaving.'

'Maria, you are my muse. I'll never finish my painting without you.'

She did not answer.

'I'll come back from the dead, if that's what you want.'

Still nothing.

'Look, here's the wretched envelope. And I'll take the Mona Lisa back. How would that be? I'll take it back and no harm done.'

'You'll take it back?' snapped Mademoiselle Leveret. 'Really? You won't forget or change your mind or say you did when you didn't?'

Monsieur X drew himself up. He looked as huffy as Monsieur du Perche. 'All right. Just for that I *will* take it back, and *you* can be on your way too. I don't need you! Go and, and, water your geraniums till they drown – and take your cat with you!'

Without another word, Mademoiselle Leveret scooped up Noir and walked out the door. Monsieur X began pulling packing materials from under the table, all injured nobility.

Granny would say they should both just stew in their own juices till they're ready to come down off their high horse, thought Slightly. But there was too much at stake for that.

She stood up.

'Well?' grunted Monsieur X. 'What do you think you're doing?'

Slightly took a deep breath. 'I'm coming with you.'

'Why? Don't you trust me either?'

'No. I don't.'

Monsieur X tipped back his head and laughed out loud.

'Clever girl,' he said.

CHAPTER THIRTEEN:
Always Night

And so it began – the strangest journey Slightly had ever made. Monsieur X handed her a coat, and even though it was too big, she was grateful for it. It might be spring in the world above, but here it was damp and cold. *And it will never change*, she thought, *because the sun never rises here. Here it is always night*. She shivered.

'The Hidden City – how big is it?' she asked, trying not to quaver. 'We can't go all the way to the Louvre underground, can we?' She was very, very keen to get back to street level.

Monsieur X shifted the bundled-up Mona Lisa onto his other shoulder and grinned at her, looking altogether evil in the lantern light.

'Oh can't we? There is more to the Hidden City than you can begin to imagine. Above ground, there are hidden rooms all over the city, behind panels, through wardrobes with false backs, reached by stairs built inside the walls, that start at the rooftop and go down past the level of the street. And below *those* streets are *other* streets – miles and miles of them – tunnels through the rock, spreading far and wide, joined by galleries and ramps and carved stone steps. How many centuries of quarrying have there been? How many tons of stone taken out? How much of Paris above ground is built out of Paris below ground? How many mines are there under the streets? These are questions I don't know the answer to. No one does.'

'That's crazy! How can you not know where there's a mine? Mines are *big*.'

Monsieur X shrugged. 'People forget. Or bits cave in, or the entrance becomes blocked, and they assume that's an end to it. But they're wrong. The tunnels snake everywhere, on different levels, following where the seams of good stone have been dug out. Like an ants' nest, with passages and chambers going up and down and along and around. Some of them are so narrow the quarrymen must have had to lie on their backs to dig.'

Slightly had hoped that Monsieur X's talking would help to keep her from thinking about being underground, but it wasn't working. The image of tunnels so small drove all the horror of her nightmare into the front of her mind. She tried to push it back.

'How do you know where you're going?' she squeaked. 'Is there a map?'

'I have a map, yes, in here.' Monsieur X tapped his head. 'One of the advantages of being an artist is being able to see shapes in your mind.'

'What happens to the people who come here and *aren't* artists?'

'They get lost.'

Slightly gulped. Even though it was chilly her hands were starting to sweat. Lost, in this maze of tunnels and galleries, wandering on and on as your light grew dimmer and dimmer until there was nothing but the dark, pressing down on you . . . She couldn't breathe properly – there were strange dots in front of her eyes –

'Oh, look at you! Steady on, steady on. Here, sit for a moment. Put your head between your

knees . . . That's it, slow breathing, slow breathing.'
Monsieur X's voice was suddenly concerned and,
Slightly realised woozily, *embarrassed*.

'Maria is going to scold me for this. I didn't mean
to scare you, child. I get carried away sometimes. It's
dangerous down here, yes, but look, there, on the
wall – see those marks? There are numbers, too, and
dates, that help you get your bearings. And sometimes
there are even street names, just like the streets above.
Folk who live in the Hidden City know how to read
those.'

*Marks. Sign posts to find your way. To get you where
you want to go and then OUT!* She started to feel a
little better. *I bet Sherlock Holmes never had dizzy fits.*

'Are you ready to stand up?' asked Monsieur X
anxiously.

Slightly heaved herself off the floor, determined
not to be childish any more. 'I'm all right. Let's go.'
She remembered something. 'Did you just say there
are people *living* down here?'

'Of course. You've driven about up there –'
he pointed over his head. 'You've seen all Baron
Haussmann's *improvements*.' He said the word as if it
tasted bad.

'I don't understand,' said Slightly.

'When Baron Haussmann cleared away the

narrow, dirty, old streets and tumble-down tenements and replaced them with his wide boulevards and fine tall buildings, do you think the poor people just moved back in? All the displaced people, where were they to go? They came to the outlying areas and when even those were too crowded, they came down here, to the old quarries and tunnels and sewers.'

Just then Monsieur X stopped talking and started to whistle. It felt too loud and it was certainly tuneless. The noise made Slightly grimace. 'Why are you doing that?'

'Not everybody who finds their way down here has good manners.'

'Whistling is good manners?'

'Of course. Lets folk know you're not trying to sneak up on them.'

'Excuse me,' came a voice behind her, and Slightly nearly leapt out of her skin as a little girl passed them, carrying two heavy buckets of water on a yoke over her thin shoulders.

'What?! Where . . . ?'

'She's been to a well, just down the passageway back there, that the old miners used – cleanest water in Paris!' said Monsieur X with pride. 'And this is where she lives.'

Ahead, thick pillars of unexcavated stone held up the roof, like the trunks of a fat stone forest. Scattered through the maze, Slightly was amazed to see makeshift hearths and sleeping places, and scenes of family life being acted out. The smoke from the fires drifted steadily along the stone ceiling towards another tunnel, following air currents she could only guess at.

Monsieur X nudged Slightly with a sharp elbow. 'Don't stare!' he hissed.

Some of the inhabitants greeted Monsieur X. Others didn't look up. But no one asked where they were going, or what was in the parcel. *Curiosity isn't good manners, either,* thought Slightly. Granny would agree with that. But she didn't want to think about Granny just then.

They carried on. Monsieur X showed her each mark they passed. 'There are different levels, dug out at different times. The marks can change when the depth does.'

Slightly had been aware of the passage they were following sloping downwards, levelling off, then tending down again. Now they turned along another tunnel that slanted sharply upwards. There were ridges gouged into the stone floor but damp had made them dangerously slippery.

'Careful,' Monsieur X cautioned.

At the top of the ramp the passageway divided into two. Monsieur X bore right, first shining the lantern on the mark on the wall for her to see.

Sherlock Holmes would have no trouble remembering all this, she thought anxiously. For her, though, the marks were all beginning to blur.

They passed many more forks and galleries and side caves, but no more people. Then Slightly realised that she'd been hearing a whooshing noise for some time without really noticing it. Now, though, it was growing steadily louder.

'Storm drains,' said Monsieur X. 'We'll be taking a boat for the next part.'

As they came to the end of the next tunnel, the whooshing became a roaring and suddenly they were on the brink of a torrent of water. A man was sitting there, staring down into the black flow and only looking up when Monsieur X tapped him repeatedly on the shoulder. There was a brief conversation – money exchanged hands – and the man untied a rickety, shallow-keeled boat from a rusted ring and handed over the rope. He didn't look at Slightly at all.

Monsieur X settled her in the bow, placed the precious bundle in her arms, and pushed off from the stern. When Slightly looked back, the man had returned to gazing at the water.

'He says it tells him stories,' said Monsieur X. 'Some day, he's going to write them down.'

Like Mr Thurgood. The thought made Slightly sad. She hugged the Mona Lisa for comfort.

They made good progress through the storm drains. Sometimes it was eerily quiet, so that Slightly heard no sound but the splash of the pole or the ripple of the water against the side of the boat. Sometimes she was deafened by the roar of waterfalls from side tunnels. Sometimes they passed under cellar bars and nightclubs, and noise and light spilled down through grills in the ceiling, raucous and harsh in the confined space. Laughter, drunken shouts, the clink of glasses. Someone crying.

Monsieur X told her to close the door of the lantern then, and they glided under the gratings in silence.

'Don't look up,' he whispered. 'Your face will show against the darkness.'

They don't know we're here, Slightly thought, looking steadily down at the bundle lying across her lap. *We don't exist.*

The journey went on and on. Eventually Monsieur X moored the boat and they continued by foot through cross tunnels and galleries. Slightly thought they must have travelled for miles, but what if all the time they'd been going round in circles, getting nowhere?

And then, just as she felt she couldn't go another step, they were there.

CHAPTER FOURTEEN:
Shadows in the Louvre

The passage ended abruptly in a blank wall. When Slightly looked closer, though, she was able to see the faint outline of a door. A range of disguises and a mirror hung from hooks along one side. A carpenter's toolbag and apron. A cleaning woman's rough dress and sacking apron. An official-looking blue-black coat with brass buttons and a guard's hat, which Monsieur X put on with practised ease, adjusting the hat to just the right angle in the mirror. He opened a box and took out something

Slightly couldn't quite see, which he popped into his mouth. When he turned around, she squeaked in surprise. It was the part-man, part-rabbit museum guard – the one who'd spoken to her the day Signor Vasarino realised the Mona Lisa was a fake. She remembered the odd look on his face.

That was when he saw Granny!

Monsieur X grinned toothily, then bent and removed his shoes, tied the laces and hung them round his neck.

'You too,' he whispered, pointing at her feet.

Slightly did as she was told reluctantly. *It's going to be cold just in my stockings*, she thought, and she was absolutely right. The flagstones of the passage made her toes curl.

Monsieur X closed the dark lantern.

'Quiet,' he whispered to her, and eased open the door in the wall, just a sliver. It seemed to Slightly he then stood for hours, barely breathing, listening intently. Whenever she shifted even a little he shot warning glances at her, but at long last he was satisfied. He drew her through the door and slid it silently shut behind them.

Slightly could feel that they had entered a tall, wide, open space. A space that the lantern, as Monsieur X cautiously opened its door, had no chance of lighting. She was in a gallery of the Louvre. As her eyes adjusted, she glimpsed looming white shapes – twisting limbs and swirling draperies, women and men and horses and monsters . . . Monsieur X took her arm and hurried through the statues without a sideways glance. Their stockinged feet made no sound on the freezing marble floor. Up a set of stairs like art-loving ghosts they flitted, along a hallway, down another flight. Slightly was utterly lost. It was like her nightmare, except there'd been decent lighting in her dream!

Monsieur X skidded to a halt so suddenly she ran right into him.

'Wha—' began Slightly, but he clamped his hand over her mouth before she could finish. He shoved the precious painting into her arms and pushed her behind a statue of four huge baboons squatting in a row with their front paws up. She fell to her knees on the hard stone floor and could barely keep from crying out, but she managed to keep the picture safe.

And then she heard it too.

The *clump, clump, clump* of heavy shoes coming towards them.

Slightly waited for Monsieur X to slide in beside her, silent and still. What he *did*, was the exact opposite.

Peering from her hiding place, she saw him shove his big shoes onto his feet – *clump, clump* – and then, as if that wasn't enough to draw attention to himself, he started whistling.

What are you doing?! she cried in silent horror. *You're not in the Hidden City now!*

She watched, mesmerised, as an approaching light flowed up the far wall, turning it an eerie flickering yellow. A statue of the lion at the top of the stairs was illuminated and for a moment the shadows in the hollows of its eyes seemed to move. They were looking straight at her.

The owner of the lantern came to the top of the stairs and stopped.

Slightly covered her face with her hands. *He's in disguise. It'll be fine. He's in disguise.* But what if the real guard saw through it? She'd have to find the right gallery and replace the painting herself – but how? Where was she now? The Louvre was so huge –

'*Bonsoir*, Monsieur,' said Monsieur X calmly. There was some chat and chuckling between them. Then the guard bid Monsieur X a pleasant goodbye and carried on his way.

Monsieur X sat down on the steps and took off his boots again. Then he beckoned to Slightly to bring him the painting.

'Come on.' And he started up the stairs.

'You got away with it,' whispered Slightly.

Monsieur X looked sideways at her and the lantern lit up the big fake teeth in his face. 'Of course. The Louvre has so many guards, there is almost always going to be somebody off ill. Or away to get married. Or visiting a sick aunt. And then good old me, the trusty reserve guard, fills in.'

He's been in and out of here who knows how many times! Her steps slowed as an awful thought rose in her mind. *How many of the paintings in the Louvre are Charles Chant copies?*

Don't think about that now, she told herself firmly and scuttled after Monsieur X's retreating lantern.

And, suddenly, they had arrived at their destination. Slightly felt the hairs on the back of her neck standing up, as if someone were behind her, watching, but every time she turned, there was no one there but the painted eyes of the long dead.

'There she is,' breathed Monsieur X. 'Perhaps my finest work.'

He lifted down the fake Mona Lisa and laid it carefully face up on the floor. Then he unwrapped the original and placed it beside the copy. He gestured to Slightly to come closer. He took out a small knife and with delicate care, marked the top of his copied painting, so that a crack appeared, identical to the crack on the original.

For a moment the two paintings were revealed, side by side, disconcerting and beautiful in the lantern light.

'They're so alike,' breathed Slightly, looking from one to the other in amazement.

'They are, aren't they. So alike that I think we could play a little game. I think if you turned your back and I shuffled the paintings about a little you wouldn't be able to tell me which one I should put up on the wall.'

He was tempted – Slightly could see it clearly on his face – he was tempted to put the forgery back up, *his* painting, hanging in the Louvre . . .

'It's an amazing work,' said Slightly. 'But I like the painting you did of Mademoiselle Leveret better.' Monsieur X turned his head abruptly and stared hard at her with a very odd expression on his face. It made her a little afraid. Then he grunted and put a hand on his side.

'What is it?' asked Slightly.

But Monsieur X shook his head and wrapped up the copy. 'Nothing. Just a touch of indigestion. I always get indigestion when I have to give back a painting without making any money from it. It feels like they won.'

'It's not a game,' said Slightly, but she didn't think Monsieur X was listening. He lifted the original painting up into its place, adjusted it a little until it was straight and turned away.

'Let's go home,' was all he said.

They left the gallery to the shadows and the silence, and the Mona Lisa's enigmatic smile.

CHAPTER FIFTEEN:
'La fissure!
La fissure!'

They walked for what felt like hours without seeing or hearing another soul. Monsieur X refused to let Slightly carry the painting, even though it was clear it was weighing him down. He walked as if he were weary and discouraged, very different from the glib, irrepressible, opinionated man who'd led them on their outward journey.

He told her they were taking a different way back. He didn't say why. Slightly hoped there might be some sitting down in a boat with this route, but he shook his head and fell silent again.

They were moving through the older parts of the Hidden City. The ceilings felt lower and some of the passageways were horribly narrow. Sometimes Slightly could hear water rushing somewhere out of sight, but then it would fade and there was only the dull echo of their footsteps to break the silence. She tried to imagine the tunnels full of ancient miners, digging, talking, living their hard lives, but it was impossible. This was a place that had been empty too long. The markings on the walls were old and strange and some of them had faded with time to little more than a smudge on the stone. Slightly kept biting her tongue to stop herself from asking, 'Do you know where we are? Is this the right way? Are you sure? Are we lost?'

Until, suddenly, Monsieur X paused and pointed. There was a mark she recognised. They had rejoined the route they'd travelled before – the way that led to Mademoiselle Leveret's cave!

'Not long now,' said Monsieur X. His voice sounded thin and strange after the silence.

Not long now. Even though she was tired to the bone, Slightly put on a burst of speed. She was desperate to escape from these endless tunnels. It was getting harder and harder to not think about all the rock overhead. Yet the more urgent these feelings became, the slower it seemed Monsieur X was walking. The painting was such a burden he was almost bent in half carrying it.

'You know,' said Slightly, 'there was a space we just passed, on the left. A little sort of side cave. We could put the painting there, for safe keeping. Just for now, I mean, and then retrieve it in the morning. It's been a long night. What do you say?' *Say yes,* she thought wearily.

Monsieur X looked as if he were about to argue, but then he changed his mind. He turned back with a shrug and propped the painting up against the wall, out of sight, just inside the entrance to the cave. 'I'll come back for it tomorrow,' he said. He straightened up, started forward along the tunnel again – then clutched at his side.

'Monsieur X!'

He looked terrible. He was sweating and his lips were blue in the lantern light. Slightly grabbed his hand, then dropped it at once with a cry. It was clammy and cold. *Like a corpse. This can't be happening. He said his heart was bad – I don't know anything about heart attacks – what am I supposed to do?*

She made herself help him slide down the wall to a sitting position on the floor and loosened his collar. She put her hand on his chest where she could feel his heart pounding. It was making his shirt move. *That's too fast. I know that's too fast.*

There was a strange, low, groaning sound, like something in pain, but oddly, it seemed to be coming from behind her. *What was that?*

'Monsieur X? Talk to me!'

But he didn't answer. He clutched at the front of her coat. He seemed to be having trouble focusing his eyes properly. Instead of looking into her face, his gaze was fixed over her shoulder.

'*La fissure . . .*' he whispered urgently. '*La fissure!*'

Slightly frowned. How was she supposed to help him if he started speaking French at her? And what was he staring at?

She tried to turn her head but it was hard to do with Monsieur X holding onto her coat so tightly.

'*Fi . . . fissure . . .*'

'You know I don't speak French, and you're starting to choke me, so just you let go and I'll have a look at what's worrying you and then I'll . . .' Slightly's words dried up in her mouth as she detached herself from Monsieur X's grip, turned her head, and understood with a horrible clarity exactly what *la fissure* meant . . .

It meant 'crack'. Like the one in the ceiling of the tunnel that hadn't been there a moment before.

It was black and gaping and as threatening as a poisonous snake. As threatening and as deadly.

'Run!' croaked Monsieur X.

'What? No! I won't leave you –'

And then it was too late.

CHAPTER SIXTEEN:
No Choice

Slightly was thrown to the ground as, with an unbearable roar, the roof collapsed. Pulverised stone crashed down, sharp-edged fragments biting into her arms, back, legs. The air became opaque with dust. She buried her head in her arms and if she screamed she couldn't hear herself over the sound of the rock falling.

Time seemed to stop as she lay there, rigid and hurting. But then, at last, she realised that the world was no longer shuddering. She was afraid to move, for fear of starting it all up again, but she knew she couldn't stay as she was forever. With infinite caution she lifted her head and was immediately convulsed with coughing as the dust in the air clogged her throat. Amazingly, miraculously, though, she could see! The lantern had escaped unbroken and the light from the candle lit the still-swirling dust-laden air eerily. For a long moment she just lay there, staring at the wonder that was light in such a place. Then she remembered Monsieur X.

He was still propped against the tunnel wall, coated all over with grey dust. He did not seem to be cut or crushed by the pieces of broken rock and he was breathing, but he wasn't opening his eyes.

'Wake up, Monsieur, wake up, please!' she whispered. Behind them, the tunnel was filled from floor to ceiling with blocks of dressed stone and jagged chunks of rock. Where there had been one collapse there could be another, and next time they might not be so lucky. 'Please? We can't stay here!'

When he didn't respond, she bent and took awkward hold of him to drag him away to safety. Very soon it was clear she wasn't nearly strong enough. There was nothing for it but to leave him behind.

'Don't you worry. I'll go for help,' she told him, still whispering. 'You rest here.' She laid him flat and tried to make him comfortable, spreading her borrowed coat over him, brushing the dust from his face as best she could. She wished he would speak to her, just a word, to reassure her. Nothing. But maybe that was for the best, since she would be taking the lantern and he would be left in the dark . . .

Time to go, she told herself firmly and dragged herself upright. Everything ached. *Come on, Slightly. Best foot forward! Don't look back.*

With a ragged breath, she limped away. *It's not that far. All I have to do is look for the marks – there! This is good. I'm going the right way. I'm going to make it.*

It was cold without a coat and she felt bruised all over but, so far, the way was straightforward . . . until she came to a place where the tunnels forked. Was this the ramp they'd climbed on the outward journey? That went steeply down to a lower level? *There.* The mark on the left-hand wall that Monsieur X had pointed out was visible in the lantern light.

She started down the left hand tunnel. Yes, here was the ramp. Carefully, she began to descend. But then, as she held the lantern up, she saw something that seemed to block the way. Something dark, that moved as if it were alive. She stared at it, unsure what it could be, but instinctively afraid. Then she realised.

Water. The tunnel was filling with water.

Slightly's heart tried to climb into her mouth. She remembered the distant thunder and the forked lightning they'd seen from the Eiffel Tower. She remembered Granny commenting on the strange stillness. *Weather's coming,* she'd said.

It *had* come, with a vengeance, while she and Monsieur X, all unaware, were on their underground errand. Innocent rain. It had never been more than a bother before now. She'd never thought about where it went after it splashed on her in the streets. She'd never thought it could kill her.

'Oh, Granny!' Slightly whispered into the silence. 'Oh Granny!'

The incline was so steep that the water was already inches from the ceiling. She could not go this way and she could not go back to Monsieur X without help. There was nothing for it but the other tunnel, unmarked, uncharted, terrifying.

Slightly climbed back up the ramp to the fork, took a deep breath and walked into the unknown. Almost at once, there was a bend in the passageway, a bend *away* from Mademoiselle Leveret's cave. It was not the direction she needed to be going, but she could only hope that soon it would bend back again. She began to go faster and faster, trying to make up the lost time. *How is Monsieur X now? Lying there in*

the cold, in the dark. I've been so long! She must get
help to him before it was too late. *Hurry – hurry!* He
could be dying at this very moment. *Please don't die
– please don't be dead.* She broke into a run –

She was up to her ankles in icy water. It was here
too! Black and evil-looking, lapping hungrily at her
feet. *Back! Go back!* her body screamed at her but
how *could* she go back?

She made herself go on, feeling with her feet for
fear that the unseen floor might suddenly drop away.
Her stockings and shoes and skirt were soaked and
heavy with the freezing water. She was shivering
uncontrollably now and she clenched her jaws so tight
they ached, trying to stop her teeth from clattering
together. The lantern reflected off the black surface
and then she strangled a scream as a huge rat swam at
her out of the gloom. Frantically she pressed herself
against the dank wall to get out of its way, but it paid
no attention to her at all and powered on down the
tunnel. She watched it until it was out of sight and
then, reluctantly, sloshed forward again.

*Even the rats are fleeing. They do that from a sinking
ship.* But this was worse than a sinking ship. In the
open ocean you could at least try to swim, but in a
tunnel, once the water got to the ceiling, there was
only drowning . . .

She had no choice; she must keep going. But it was almost more than she could do to force herself forward. The water was rising, she was sure of that now. Even in the few moments she'd stood still, it had crept its icy fingers further up her legs. Could she still wade through? Slightly raised the lantern as high as she could, but the tunnel curved sharply to the right so she couldn't see how far it was flooded. She shuffled forward a little. Her chest hurt as if she were already running out of air. *I can't be trapped. I can't. This can't be where I'm going to die –*

She hit the wall with her hand in desperate frustration.

'No! No – nooooo!'

Her despairing cry echoed strangely along the tunnel – echoed against the stone ceiling and walls, changing, oddly, into another cry altogether –

'*Nooowwwarrrllll!*'

Slightly held her breath, listening hard. A wild hope welled up inside her.

'*Noowarrlll?*'

There it was again!

'Noir? Noir – is it you?' Her voice croaked. 'Are you there?' Now she was splashing forward, steadying herself against the wall. 'Noir?'

'*Nwwarrlll!*'

The curve of the passage went on and on. She could feel the water trying to slow her down, hold her back. She pressed forward against it and almost fell. Was it straightening? Was the water getting shallower? There seemed to be a definite upward slope. The lantern light reflected off two small, round discs of yellow in the darkness up ahead . . . and there she was.

Noir the cat. Sitting upright with her tail wrapped gracefully around her paws, just beyond the reach of the water. Waiting for Slightly, as if it were the most normal thing in the world, instead of the most miraculous.

Slightly sobbed, desperate to run, but she forced herself to move slowly and carefully so that there would be no tidal wave or splashes to disturb that elegant small figure. *She must have come along the tunnel so it must lead somewhere safe. It must lead OUT!*

Slightly stepped from the water, scooped the cat into her arms and kissed the top of its head.

'You came to get me, you wonderful moggie. I will buy you every fish in the market and buckets of cream and I'll get Monsieur X to paint your portrait because you are the most beautiful cat in all of Paris and I'll make Monsieur du Perche hang it in the Louvre, right beside the Mona Lisa.' She was crying in earnest now and salt tears dripped down onto Noir's fur, so Slightly put her down, gently, as if she were made of glass.

'Now, lead on. And please, dear cat, hurry!'

She wanted more than anything to rush away in search of a grown-up and hand all the horror over. But she realised it was no good getting help for Monsieur X if the help couldn't *find* him. She made herself hold up the lantern at each junction they came to and write the marks on the walls into her notebook. She made herself count paces and left turns and right turns as Noir the cat led the way, as confidently as if she were walking across the rooftops of Paris, high, high above. When Slightly stopped, she stopped too and groomed her leg or behind her ears with her paw until it was time to move on again.

All the while, Slightly's brain kept shouting at her, worrying and wailing.

It's taking too long . . . we should have got there by now . . . somewhere, anywhere . . . how do I know Noir knows where she's going? She's just a cat . . . what do I do if she disappears? . . . what do I do if the passage is blocked and there's only a cat-sized way through and she goes on without me and I'm trapped . . . trapped . . . trapped . . .

Then it happened. Noir ran ahead, round a bend, and out of sight.

CHAPTER SEVENTEEN:
Meeting of the Muses

With a cry, Slightly raced after the cat, all the horrors she'd been trying to suppress breaking free inside her chest.

And there it was: the door to Mademoiselle Leveret's cave, with Noir sitting expectantly by, waiting to be let in.

Slightly fumbled with the latch and half-fell into the golden glow of the firelight.

'Miss Jones!' Mademoiselle Leveret started up from her chair. 'What has happened?'

'You, you're here! You came back!'

'Yes, I'm sorry, my behaviour was so bad, but please, you must tell me *what has happened*?!'

For one long moment, Slightly couldn't speak. She'd forgotten even how to breathe. She just stood there with her mouth opening and shutting like a fish, staring as the blood drained from Maria's face.

'Please, my dear,' Mademoiselle Leveret said. 'Please tell me.'

Slightly took a great gulp of air, and began to talk. When she finished Mademoiselle Leveret took her notebook from her, asked a very few questions, and was gone.

Slightly looked around the empty room, collapsed into Maria's chair and found she was crying again. Noir the cat said, '*Nwarlll*?' leapt onto her lap and let Slightly hug her, in spite of the wetness of tears.

She didn't know how long she sat there, but at last she gave one final sniff and told herself, as firmly as she could manage, *That's quite enough of that. Get a grip, Slightly! Sherlock Holmes wouldn't be sitting about, weeping all over a cat.*

She got up, feeling chilled and wobbly, and went to Mademoiselle Leveret's washing stand. She dabbed at her face with the cold water, but only managed to spread the dirt about. When she tried to run a comb through her hair it snagged impossibly. *Granny is going to scold me something awful,* she thought and then, just as tears threatened *again,* suddenly Mademoiselle Leveret's cave was alarmingly full of strangers, including a strong man carrying Monsieur X in his arms as gently as if he were a sick child. The little of him she could see was caked in grey dust. She couldn't tell if his chest was moving.

'Is he dead?'

'Not yet. If we hadn't found him . . .' As Maria hurriedly gathered up some blankets and banked the fire, Slightly could see she was white with worry but holding it fiercely in check. 'And now we must take him up.'

The men exchanged uneasy glances and edged for the door.

'We must take him up,' repeated Mademoiselle Leveret in a voice that cracked part way through. 'Please,' she added more softly. 'Take him to my room above and then I will do nothing until you are safely away again. I can't let him die here, I must get a doctor, I must save him . . .'

The strong man finally nodded. As Maria led the way along the passage Slightly kept repeating to herself, *He's still alive. He's still alive!* and then, sooner than she was expecting, they were back in the meeting of the tunnels where she'd first entered the Hidden City.

It seemed a lifetime ago.

Now they began the long climb back up the tightly-spiralling stone steps. Slightly's legs burned and she was sobbing for breath. How the man carrying Monsieur X was managing she couldn't imagine.

'Shhhh . . .' The sound hissed down from above. 'Quiet!

They had reached the top of the secret stairs. Mademoiselle Leveret shifted a concealed lever, the hidden door slid open, early morning sunlight exploded into the small space –

And there was Granny, a ferocious expression on her face and a poker in her hand.

'What have you done with Slightly?' she demanded.

Slightly stumbled forward, gasping, 'I'm here! I'm here!'

'Are you all right? You look terrible!'

'Yes, Granny, I'm fine – it's just the dust from the cave-in. I found Mademoiselle Leveret and we put the Mona Lisa back, just in time – but Monsieur X has had some sort of heart attack and needs a doctor, except he isn't Monsieur X, he's your Mr Chant.'

'What? Who? How . . .?'

Granny blinked several times, her makeshift weapon drooping in her hand, until Mademoiselle Leveret stepped forward and gently took the poker away from her.

'It's all right,' said Slightly. 'I'll explain later.'

'You certainly will,' said Granny. She took a deep breath, turned on her heel and went out onto the house landing. Leaning over the balustrade, she called down to the room below, 'Mr Westerly, fetch a doctor, please. Ask Madame Bec to direct you.'

Slightly couldn't hear his response but Granny called back, 'No, our girl is fine and I haven't time to tell you more. The doctor, as quick as you can.' The clatter of Mr Westerly's shoes on the stairs were clear enough, though.

Granny returned briskly. 'If you would please put the sick gentleman down on Mademoiselle's bed,' she said to the man. 'And then I am sure I will find I have no idea how he got there.'

There was a small flurry of activity as the strong man's burden was settled onto Maria's bed, but Slightly wasn't paying attention. After so long underground, she found herself entranced by the rich colour of the geraniums in the window. She pushed open the window and took deep gulps of the early morning air.

It's blue, she thought, looking up. *The sky is still blue.*

'*Merci*, Monsieur, and *au revoir*,' Mademoiselle Leveret was saying, but as Slightly turned back into the room it was already too late to add her thanks or farewells. The hidden door had already sighed shut again, and Slightly could see no seam or crack to show where it had been.

'Where am I?' A weak voice came from the bed. 'Where have you brought me?'

Maria turned to Granny. 'I will go and ask Madame Bec for some restoratives. Now that he has returned to himself, it is important he stays awake. Can you do that, Madame? Keep him talking until the doctor arrives?'

'I think I can manage to do that. We are old friends. And it's not Madame. It's Mademoiselle.'

Mademoiselle Leveret nodded and hurried out.

'Lily? Is that you?'

'Yes, you old fool. It's me.' Granny settled herself by the bed.

'Oh, Lily, I couldn't believe my eyes when I saw you in the Louvre – in Paris again after all this time.'

'And there *I* was, thinking you were dead. I even put flowers on your grave.'

'I nearly was, this time. It was your girl who got me saved?'

Granny looked over at Slightly and nodded proudly. 'Yes. It was my girl.'

'I'll paint her portrait,' wheezed Mr Chant. 'To say thank you. It'll be such a wonder, they'll –'

'I know, they'll hang it in the Louvre,' interrupted Granny. 'You always used to say that.'

Mr Chant chuckled hoarsely and then began to cough. Granny helped him sip some water.

'Do you remember what we used to talk about,' he continued, 'while you were pretending to copy paintings at the Louvre? And I was pretending to do the same even though all I was really doing was trying to copy you?'

'I remember we talked a lot of rubbish,' said Granny sharply, but then her voice softened. 'Pleasant rubbish, though. I remember it was always that.'

'I was going to get away from Paris and go find somewhere warm. I always liked the sound of the Limpopo River.'

And there it was. The answer to the mystery that Slightly had wondered about for all those years. But Mr Chant was still speaking.

'I always thought I'd like to paint that river. And you, sitting on the bank! You were my muse, Lily. I was devastated when you went back to England like that.'

'Devastated?' snorted Granny. 'For how long?'

Mr Chant shrugged and spread his hands. 'Weeks! I swear! But then, well, you wouldn't have wanted me to stop painting *for ever*, would you?'

Slightly watched Granny. *Is she going to be angry? Is she going to be sad?* she wondered. Then Granny laughed out loud, which was *not* what she was expecting.

'No. No, my dear Charles, I would not want you to stop painting. Not even for a day.'

Just then Mademoiselle Leveret came back into the room, clutching smelling salts and a tonic. Granny looked over her shoulder and smiled, and Slightly suddenly felt sure it was going to be all right between them.

But would Monsieur X's heart be all right?

The two muses stepped out of the room to speak together and for a moment, Slightly was too weary to move. But then she forced herself to walk quietly over to the bed. *Keep him talking*, Maria had said.

'Mr Chant? Are you better?'

To be honest, he looked terrible, with grey rock dust clogging his hair and coating his skin. But his voice, when he spoke, was sounding stronger already. Almost back to normal.

'Yes. Much better.'

'Well enough to answer a question?'

'Always questions! Ask then, Miss Detective Jones.'

'Was that true, that you wanted to take Granny to the Limpopo?'

'Yes, quite true. Why?'

'Oh, nothing. Only, do you know how people in Britain sometimes name their houses after things that are important to them?'

The man on the bed nodded.

'Granny named *her* house Limpopo.'

CHAPTER EIGHTEEN:
Full Moon Again

Signor Vasarino's private viewing of the real Mona Lisa was a complete success, and Madame Mini flattered him outrageously right up to the moment he returned to Italy.

'You did an excellent job,' said Slightly.

'Maybe,' said Madame Mini with one of her shrugs. 'But next time, *no one* is going to keep me away from the real excitement!'

In fact, Monsieur du Perche was surprised to find his wife now spending much of her time in and around his grand office.

He was even more surprised to find her quickly becoming indispensable.

'I do not choose to be lonely any more,' Madame Mini told Slightly, and then she added in a whisper, 'And also, I am on the lookout for more mysteries!'

But what to do about the notorious Monsieur X or, as Slightly must now get used to calling him, Mr Charles Chant? The Trustees at the Louvre were not going to publicise the incident with the Mona Lisa, of course, but what about all the money he owed, that had prompted his pretend death in the first place?

'When you are well again, perhaps I will commission you to paint my portrait,' suggested Madame Mini. 'What would you charge?'

And Mr Chant, with a charming smile, told her.

It was an *outrageous* sum, which just happened to be exactly the amount needed to pay off all of his debts . . .

'You are a naughty man,' said Madame Mini, and gave him the money.

Mr March invited Mr Chant and his niece to come and stay in his large flat for the foreseeable future. Mademoiselle Leveret was in this way able to look after her uncle as he convalesced and help Mr March in both his studios as well.

Mr March and Mr Chant got on surprisingly well, especially after all the ransom money Mr March had scraped together was returned to him. Mr Chant asked, though, if he could keep the sketch he'd stolen from Slightly's pocket, and Mr March had said yes, with a pleased look on his face. Maria sat quietly mending or reading or stroking Noir the cat (who still disappeared from time to time, but always returned to her chosen human) and the two men talked about art, illustrating their points with scribbles on scraps of paper.

'Mademoiselle Leveret gives them courage, I think,' said Mr Westerly to Slightly.

'Do you think they'll be able to share her? *Can* you be a muse to two people at the same time?'

'Oh yes.'

And Slightly had to accept that he would know. She couldn't help wondering, though, if Mr Westerly felt the need for a muse too.

'Would you like to stay with them?' she asked. She was afraid of the answer, but she had to know.

'Stay here? In Paris? Oh no. I've a full sketchbook and as many ideas as my head can safely hold. I'm ready to get back to my own studio!'

Slightly looked at Mr Westerly's moustache, just to be sure, and it was true! He – and it – were full of vim and vigour and keen to be home again.

Everyone came to the Gare du Nord to see them off – Madame Mini and Mademoiselle Leveret, Madame Bec and Mr March and Mr Chant – even Monsieur du Perche took a little time away from the Louvre to wave goodbye.

Slightly stood in the midst of all the noise and crowds and chaos and thought about what a time it had been – her most frightening, exhilarating case yet! And after the detectiving was over, there had been Paris to explore. Whenever Granny started to say it was time to leave, Madame Mini would remember something else that they *must* see. They had taken a boat trip along the Seine, walked in the gardens where the trees were all turning that special spring green, climbed the towers of Notre Dame to visit the gargoyles, browsed the book stalls along the embankment, and had a spectacularly expensive lunch at a restaurant on the Eiffel Tower, looking out over the city. (No one suggested a tour of the sewers or a visit to the underground Catacombs, for which Slightly was grateful.) At the end of the month, her head was packed full of paintings and buildings and statues and cafes and museums . . . It might not be London, but Slightly was happy to admit that Paris really was, as

Madame Mini said, 'Like no other place.'

Now Slightly was well and truly ready to go home. As they waited for their luggage to be stowed, she noticed Monsieur du Perche draw Mr Chant to one side. He seemed to have something on his mind.

I wonder what? she thought. She checked to see if Granny was watching her. But, no, Granny was busy counting suitcases and valises, so Slightly edged closer, in time to overhear the Trustee say quietly, 'Is it true that your frighteningly excellent copy of the Mona Lisa is now buried forever under the streets of Paris?'

'Alas, yes. That is the case,' Mr Chant replied.

'And – I'm sure, of course – there are no *other* copies, of any *other* paintings, to be discovered . . . ?'

'Oh, Monsieur du Perche,' said Mr Chant in his most sincere, most charming voice. 'How could you think such a thing?'

Monsieur du Perche seemed relieved but as he turned to speak to Granny, Mr Chant looked over at Slightly and gave her a sly little wink.

The train was about to leave – the whistle blew – they all clambered aboard and leaned from the carriage window to wave goodbye.

'Come back and see me some day, Miss Jones,' Mr Chant called out. 'I owe you a portrait. It would be my pleasure – you've got some decent bones in that face.'

Granny laughed. 'Slightly? Sit still long enough to be painted? Not likely.'

And Slightly had to agree.

'Goodbye! Goodbye! *Au revoir*!'

⁕

The moon had waned and waxed while they had been away, and now it was full again. It hung in a calm, clear sky, lighting up the deck of the steamer, the gentle swell of the sea and the tall Dover cliffs that were just coming into view.

Granny and Slightly leaned on the railing. This time Granny was nibbling a ginger biscuit with a determined look on her face.

'I still hate ginger,' she muttered. 'But I hate seasickness more.'

There had been no more adventures. The train didn't explode, but arrived in time for an orderly embarking onto the steam packet at Calais. There were no hurricanes or pirates in evidence as they headed out across the dark waters of the Channel. Mr Westerly retired to his cabin and was now sound asleep. And Slightly and Granny were watching

Dover's white cliffs growing larger in the moonlight.

'Granny?' said Slightly.

'Yes?'

'Are you sad you didn't go with Mr Chant, back when you were young? To the Limpopo?' Slightly asked, looking at Granny out of the corner of her eyes. She was aware of a jagged lump in her chest, though she wasn't sure why.

'Of course,' said Granny. 'And of course not.' She gave Slightly a smile and a hug. 'Life's a mystery and there are lots of solutions.'

Slightly thought about that for a moment.

'Don't look so worried,' said Granny. 'You *love* mysteries.'

It was true. All the most exciting things that had ever happened to Slightly had started with the words 'I'll take the case!'

I do love mysteries! I do!

And who knew what remarkable, perplexing, *excellent* new case was waiting just around the corner? Whatever it was, Detective Slightly Jones had her hero, Mr Sherlock Holmes, to look up to, her Granny and her friends to lend a hand, and her notebook and silver propelling pencil poised.

She was ready!

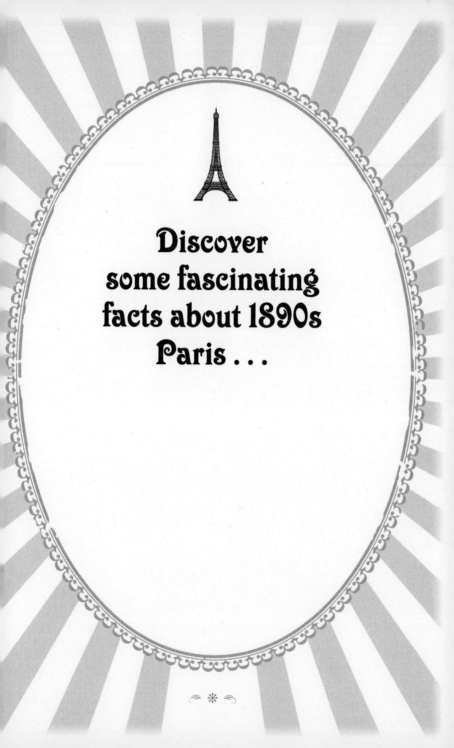

Discover
some fascinating
facts about 1890s
Paris . . .

Did you know...

...the Eiffel Tower was meant to be temporary?

The Eiffel Tower (the tallest structure in the world from 1889 right up until 1930) was built for the 1889 World's Fair in Paris. It was going to be dismantled after twenty years but, over a hundred years later, it's still standing and is visited by more than six million people from all over the world every year.

... not everybody loved the Tower at first?

There was even a petition to stop it being built:
We, writers, painters, sculptors, architects and passionate devotees of the hitherto untouched beauty of Paris, protest with all our strength, with all our indignation in the name of slighted French taste, against . . . this useless and monstrous Eiffel Tower!'
One famous author used to eat lunch at one of the Tower's restaurants regularly because he said it was the only place in Paris where he didn't have to look at it!

Paris Quiz

Test your knowledge of 1890s and modern-day Paris with these questions . . .

Slightly never visited the Catacombs – she'd had enough of being underground! But they are one of the wonders of Paris. When the city's cemeteries became too full in the eighteenth century, the bones of many Parisians were carried down to the tunnels and galleries of the old underground quarries. By the time the job of relocation was finished, it was estimated that there were

      a)   6,000

      b)   600,000

      c)   6,000,000

people interred under the streets of Paris. Which is the right number?

Three massive obelisks were given away by the Egyptian authorities during the nineteenth century. One is in Paris' Place de la Concorde, one is on the banks of the Thames in London, and the third is in new York City. Even though they were each called "Cleopatra's Needle" they were already 1000 years old when the famous Egyptian queen came to power.

TRUE OR FALSE?

a) The popular nineteenth-century travel guide, Murray's Handbook to Paris, tells us that 'in the Boulevart Neuf a building near the Barriere d'Enfer suddenly sunk down into a hole 80 ft. deep, which created great alarm, and called public attention to the subject.' He goes on to say that there's no need to worry, though, because 'the whole subterranean region' has been mapped since the cave-in.

b) Today many people travel to Paris from Britain by train, going through the Channel Tunnel. The first proposal for a Channel Tunnel was put forward early in the twentieth century.

c) Because photography is so good now, the tradition of artists copying the masterpieces in the Louvre has mostly died out.

d) The Mona Lisa has never been stolen.

e) Paris used to be completely under water.

f) In one of Sherlock Holmes' cases, he speaks of "the curious incident of the cat in the night time."

The different departments of the Louvre have exhibited their collections in lots of different rooms over the years, so it won't be possible to follow the route of Slightly's midnight visit exactly. However, if you do ever visit the Louvre see if you can find . . .

* The Mona Lisa – it's usually got a huge crowd of people in front of it, so you have to be patient!
* The Winged Victory
* Four Egyptian cats sitting in a row
* The four big baboons with their paws up that Slightly hid behind

Do you know what these French words and phrases mean?

* Le mal de mer
* La cité cachée
* Bonjour
* Au revoir
* La fissure
* Reconnaissez-vous cette dame?

The Slightly Jones Mysteries Quiz

Have you had a chance to read all of Slightly's adventures?
See how well you know the four books of the series!

Granny Tonic's Sayings

In which book did Granny say the following:
a) 'It is wisest to strike while the toast is hot.'
b) 'I'm not having you fall on your head on the train tracks. It's bad manners!'
c) 'Granny is watching you.'
d) 'They should both just stew in their own juices till they're ready to come down off their high horse.'
e) 'I'm always at home to interesting people.'
f) 'I hate ginger!'

Each of these objects plays an important role in one of Slightly's cases. Do you know which book each one is from?

The lodgers at Limpopo House are an interesting lot! What do they do when they're not helping Slightly solve mysteries?

Miss Sally Forth, Mr Reginald Westerly, Mr Malcolm Gentler, Mr Earnest Thurgood which one is:

* musician
* novelist
* translator
* artist
* night watchman

In which books do these characters appear:

Mrs Mull
Mellifluous Sprottle
North Canalbank (otherwise known as Jane)
Araminta du Perche
Frederick Twist
Octavian Snit
Morbley

The answers to The Paris Quiz and The Slightly Jones Mysteries Quiz can be found on the author's website:
www.joanlennon.co.uk

A SLIGHTLY JONES MYSTERY
The Case of the London Dragonfish

Slightly Jones has red hair, too many freckles and a flyaway temper, but she's not going to let that stop her from becoming the next Sherlock Holmes . . .

A precious fossil is about to be presented to Queen Victoria at the Natural History Museum in London. But when the exhibit goes missing the finger points to an innocent man. Slightly Jones won't let the real culprit get away with it – and, with the help of Granny Tonic, Slightly is determined to save the day.

A SLIGHTLY JONES MYSTERY
The Case of the Glasgow Ghoul

There's been a series of mysterious thefts from the Hunterian Museum in Glasgow. Despite maximum security measures, the thief is yet to be caught and the stolen objects appear to vanish into thin air, never to be seen again.

But Slightly Jones, detective-in-training, isn't daunted by the lack of clues. She's more concerned about the stories of ghosts in a nearby graveyard . . . Could the two be connected?

A SLIGHTLY JONES MYSTERY
The Case of the Cambridge Mummy

An ancient curse has been let loose in
cold, wintry Cambridge. Priceless artefacts
are found mysteriously crushed to dust at the
Fitzwilliam Museum, long-dead Egyptian
queens stalk the corridors of Girton College –
but what do bicycles and bloomers have
to do with it all?

Slightly Jones is faced with her most
bewildering case yet – and her most
ruthless opponents. Can she find the
answer in time, or will it be
a bleak midwinter for
everyone?

━ ✳ ━

You can find out more about other
exciting Catnip books by visiting:

www.catnippublishing.co.uk